My Husband

Wants

to Keep Me

Pristine

Sam Wicker

Books by Sam Wicker

I'm No Hero Trilogy
I'm No Hero
I'm Your Hero
I'm His Hero (2026)

The My Husband Wants Series
My Husband Wants to Keep Me Pristine
My Husband Wants to Keep Me Dominant (soon)
My Husband Wants to Keep Me Gay (soon)
My Husband Wants to Keep Me Sated (soon)

Standalones
The Bell Earth Witch

Sam Wicker
My Husband
Wants to
Keep Me
Pristine
Book 1 of the My Husband Wants Series

Dedication

To those who prefer to laugh instead of cry, and those who need an escape.

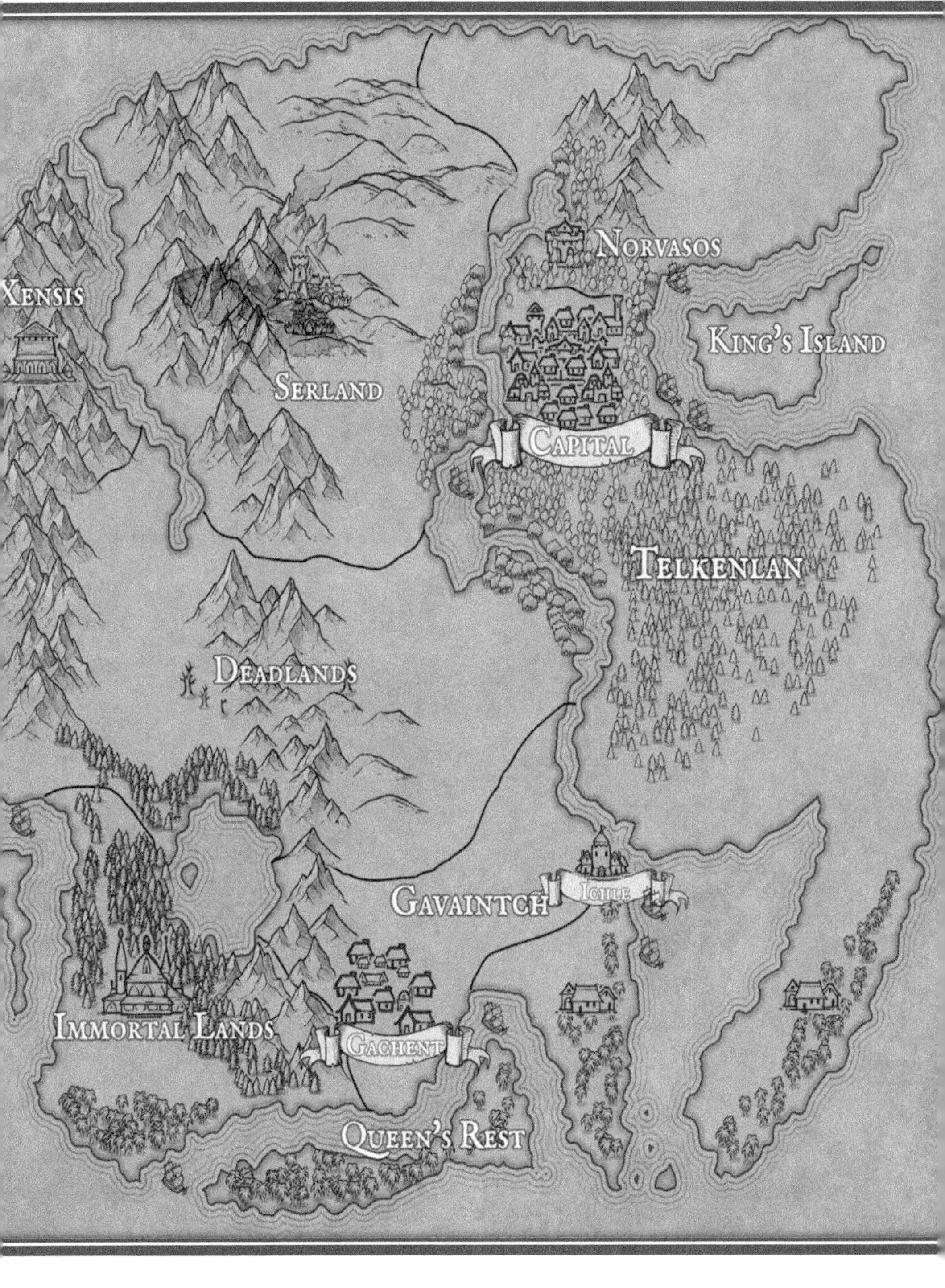

Xensis
Serland
Norvasos
King's Island
Capital
Telkenlan
Deadlands
Gavaintch
Ichle
Immortal Lands
Gachent
Queen's Rest

Chapter 1
Things That Were, Things That Are, and Some Things Are Co~~um~~ming

Accomplishment followed the delightful thumping sound of a book closing; even when she didn't want the story to end. Virsin never did. But it also meant she could move on to the next raunchy romance she wasn't supposed to read.

With much mental effort, she made herself rise from the chaise in her bedroom to hide the book in the basket next to the door under a pile of unfinished embroidery. Her maid would find it and replace it with a new one before lunch. She had a few hours to work off the extravagant breakfast she had taken in her rooms instead of with the family. Who wanted to be with family when there was a swoon-worthy romantic scene between the guard and his mistress before they eloped and lived happily ever after?

Not Virsin.

She glanced at the clock on her white mantel over the cooling coals amid gray ash. Perfect timing as her family took their walk in the garden. If she wasn't reading, the garden was the next best thing. Virsin smoothed her cream-colored dress, adjusted the lace at her chest, and then made her debut to the rest of the house. Meandering through the plush carpeted hall covered in pastoral paintings, she imagined a scene in each that would make anyone blush.

Virsin passed the double doors leading to the garden and had one foot in the marble foyer before she realized. She raked a few fingers through her brown hair, mentally shaking her head at herself. None of the scenes she imagined held her, but a slightly better version of her. A touch thinner, one or two less slanted teeth of the three, brighter eyes of blue or green was her vision of her dream self. There was nothing to be done for her plainness, but she knew she was who she needed to be.

She was the middle child of House Thesseolossos, counts they were, and as such she had one job: to be perfect enough to gain fortune through marriage for her line. There were further conditions to being 'perfect' of course. She couldn't be as perfect as her eldest sister, nor as carefree as her youngest. Condition two: she shouldn't look twice at the friends of her eldest brother, and must completely ignore the companions of her youngest brother. She was to be her elder siblings' support, and the teacher to her younger ones. A middle child wasn't supposed to be seen until the eldest were married either.

It was terrible to be a middle child.

Entering the garden, she paused under the sunlight, long enough for a cloud to cover the sun and ruin her moment. She sighed, then listened. To the east were giggles, and a clink of porcelain. Debating on whether she wanted to walk in peace, or have a snack, took a few minutes. She decided on the snack.

Within the rather extravagant garden was a gazebo grand enough to hold a table for tea for ten. Virsin watched her family at the table within the airy confines as she approached from the western path of flat stones with rich grass between. Birds sang, drowning out some of her family's voices, until she touched the bottom step.

"Sister! Tell her she's being an imbecile!" The eldest daughter, Enma, set her teacup on her saucer, her brown eyes darting to the 'imbecile' and holding there.

Virsin climbed the rest of the stairs, taking in the scene. The youngest daughter, Chuar, barely eight in years, held two chunks of dark chocolate in her hands. Evidence of pieces already devoured were at the corners of her butterfly shaped lips. "I see no imbecile, but a child eating too many sweets," she said with a smile, before glancing at their mother. She sat as if there wasn't another in the world besides her, sipping her tea with pinky curled free, a straight back and head held high.

"I haven't had a piece yet," the youngest son, but second youngest of the Thesseolossos children, shot a glare at the girl.

Gistre Thesseolossos was brown haired like the rest of them, but he had green eyes. Gistre was the closest in looks to their father, the only one to show a hint of their father's blue hued eyes amid the sea of brown. At ten, there were thirteen-year-old girls plotting their marriage with him already. How perfect.

"Have mine," Virsin took the piece off her plate and placed it on his. She smiled when he grabbed it up with a grin of thanks and popped the whole thing in his mouth.

"I am glad you are taking your diet seriously, this time, sister," Enma said with a smile over the edge of her teacup, as if she had won a battle.

They were using the set covered in lavender and roses, Enma's favorite. Virsin then knew she'd made a mistake. The tea would be horrid, burned, as Enma was a terrible tea maker and snack selector. "Are you never going to hold your own at your house?" She had to ask, forgoing the act of sipping the tea for a small muffin instead.

Who wanted muffins of prune?

She made a face, but bit into it anyway.

"My drawing room still desperately needs refurnishing. The merchant is taking his time to get my order to me. Something about a silly little storm." Enma flipped her fingers dismissively after setting her tea down. "And my garden is still full of mud."

The 'silly little storm' was the reason her sister's estate was half flooded, and why there wasn't a spot of sun in a week, until today. "How dreadful," Virsin said, but lacked commitment to the words.

"Ah, Sin, my love." Her mother acknowledged her with a pinched smile. Better late than ignored, Virsin supposed.

"Yes, Mother?" It must be something horrid poised to come out of those thin red lips, or it was something her mother was excited about. The latter could still be terrorizing. Her mother only spoke to her to give her bad advice, tell her to go to a boring engagement, or her choices of suitor for the season.

"Your father has found you a suitable husband. We are awaiting his arrival from the war. As soon as he sets foot in the near vicinity, we are to rush you to the church to marry him."

Horrible indeed. Virsin pictured a war-torn face of sun weathered flesh, a mouth missing teeth, and a body of hardness with a voice of harsh verbiage if anything ever came of it other than grunts. She floundered for words, but was relieved of speaking as Enma spoke up with a wicked smile.

"Duke Victory, my sister, is a war hero and a duke!"

Duke Victory? She had heard of him. Newly appointed to dukedom, with loose blood ties to the current king, and a male who every other man desired to be. For he was spoken of in the highest regard, even by the king and queen. Stories of his victories were epic, full of unbelievable feats like one swing of his sword tearing ten men in half. He was a human, no dragonkin blood, or anything similar, but he could still do such a thing?

"Yes, Duke Victory. I believe his real name is... oh what was it..." Her mother's voice trailed off as her eyes drifted away from her middle daughter to the tree line near the little waterway skirting the perimeter of the clearing. "Lythaine demanded your father make the deal for you. I suppose she wants you at the castle more often than you are now."

Lythaine was the queen, her cousin, and her dearest and only friend. Virsin felt the weight around her shoulders and heart lift to a comfortable level. Lythie wouldn't demand she marry someone foul and ill tempered. Would she?

"Ah, Regus something-or-other Norvasos!" Her mother returned her gaze, victorious with her memory working.

She tried her new name on her tongue, "Virsin Norvasos."

"Duchess Virsin Norvasos, dear," her mother grinned, a moment of rare animation, "I couldn't ask for a better title."

Chapter 2
Endowments Are Accessories

"Do you want to look like a snowman? Come on, let's find something better. I never in my life…" Enma kept talking as she flitted from one side to the other of the tailor's shop.

Virsin looked at the tailor, Bella, and held back another sigh. How she wished, for the hundredth time, Lythaine wasn't queen and could be here to help her choose the wedding dress and decide on the adjustments. Enma was a poor excuse for a maid of honor, but she had no other choice. She had few friends.

Those she did have, other than Lythaine, were more likened to acquaintances. The ladies of the court didn't admire the middle children. After all, they would not marry well, not have a thing special about them, why befriend a middle child for nothing? Except, Virsin was a middle child and landed a duke. What was wrong with Duke Victory to relegate him to her hand?

Nevertheless, Enma had at least five ladies simpering at her side during her wedding preparations. Enma had the fortune to marry the third in line should anything happen to the slew of children the current rulers had.

Bella helped her out of the dress and into the next one. The poor tailor had it rough. She'd already had to make or let out dresses for Virsin's frame, and now she had to deal with Enma. She wondered if her mother would mind sending a little extra money Bella's way for the trouble.

The new dress fit her like a glove. All satin and lace. Assuredly the most expensive one yet. She gritted her teeth, ready for the onslaught from Enma once her sister turned around to look.

Nothing happened. No sound. Virsin looked up from studying herself in the mirror to see if her sister was still in the dressing room part of the store. Turning slightly on the tailor's step riser so she could peer behind her. There Enma was. Her brows were toward her hairline, top eyelashes nearly meeting them, and a smile appeared.

Terrifying.

"Enma?"

"It's perfect!" Enma clapped her hands, then brought her fingers to her lips as she clasped them together.

What was the word for more than terrifying? Should she faint? She worked some words out of her brain and upon her tongue, "Are you sure? Isn't it... a bit much?"

"Pfft." Enma shook her head as she circled, reminiscent of a carrion bird.

She looked back at herself. Her tits were to her chin, flat stomach as if she didn't have one at all, ass felt like it was in a vice, and she was confident if she tried to walk, she would fall flat on her face. "Can we let it out a bi-"

"No! It's perfect."

"Enma, I can't walk." Virsin tugged a little on the dress at her hips, trying to loosen the fabric around her thighs.

"Small steps, sister. Besides, you cannot run away." Enma said, smoothing the satin covered lace before clapping her hands before her again.

Obviously. Virsin settled on that realization, biting back the urge to reveal her worry, then thought of something. "Enma, I will need some shoes, then. And gloves."

Enma nodded, "I'll be right back."

She waited until her sister walked out into the shop area before trying to get closer to Bella. Bending wasn't happening, so she whispered as loud as she dare, "Can we let it..." When Bella started nodding and beginning to mark the seams with a few pins, Virsin sighed in relief.

"My lady, I recommend leaving the torso as it is. It shows off your delightful qualities the best." Bella whispered back conspiratorially with a small smile.

"That doesn't matter. I'm marrying someone who has only seen sinful women, if any at all. I don't think he will care if I'm naked or looking like a snowman." Virsin knew in her bones it was true. After all, the man hadn't met her. She doubted her appearance would please him in any case.

"You are to wed Duke Victory, correct, my lady?"

She tilted her head in acknowledgement, "I am."

Bella asked, "Have you not heard the stories?"

She thought for a moment, "Only how he felled ten men in one strike of his sword, and how he and his seven best can do the damage of a hundred, just themselves."

"Ah, yes, those are fine tales. But, my lady, those are not all. I've heard the seven of them are easy on the eyes. Duke Victory is supposed to be ranked third in looks in the entire country. Did you not know that?" Bella insisted as she helped Virsin out of the dress.

She smiled, knowing full well the only reason the ranks of handsomeness existed was to help ease the blow of the ladies being married to those of a less-than-ideal appearance. Duke Victory was third for his wealth, power, and strategic mind, not at all for his appearance, she was sure of it.

"I see. Do what you think is best, then." Virsin knew she would not win, and she didn't have the fortitude to fight.

She needed to save her energy for the latest novel.

"Ah, darling sister," the eldest son, Blunk, greeted her as soon as the carriage door opened.

Virsin's energy drained well before she found escape in the carriage. After the tailors, Enma insisted they shop for more things for her to rise to the Duchess rank, then demanded they have tea together before Virsin was allowed to return home. Blunk's smiling face did little to raise her spirits. "Brother, to what do I owe the honor of being greeted like this?"

"I have news." Blunk said, taking her hand and helping her out. He placed her fingers around his arm, their footfalls crunching over the white gravel to the stairs leading to the double front doors of red.

She studied him in her peripheral vision. They shared the same brown hues in hair, eyes and in having the darkest skin of the siblings. It was Blunk and she who spent most of their time out in the gardens; he in training and riding, and she in reading and practicing sword play.

The latter was their secret.

"Are we in need of moving our dates, then?" She felt her heart break; it wouldn't be long before her brother couldn't tutor her.

"I'm afraid I cannot train you any longer." He turned to her midway up the stairs and grasped her shoulders. "Your husband is nigh. The ceremony is set for next week."

Chapter 3
No Means No Means No

"I don't need this."

Doxy looked at the shirt in his hands, then back to his lord. "Um, but you do, sir."

Regus met Doxy's dark brown eyes in the mirror, watching the boy fidget. He could almost read the thoughts running through behind those eyes. "If I show up half-naked, surely her family, even the queen herself, would call off the wedding. Don't you think?" He wasn't about to ride in the capital without pants, shirtless, maybe. Especially if it got him out of the current mess.

He bit back the smirk as Doxy mentally flailed, evidenced by his multitude of half started words and flushed face. Regus shook his head, turned and held his arms down and forward. "Shirt."

Doxy immediately pulled the sleeves over Regus' hands and the shirt up over his head, which he had to bend to let the boy do. The fabric fell on his broad shoulders and he helped Doxy smooth it down to his waist. The boy made quick work of the laces, tightening them and tying them off. Then the jacket was in Doxy's hands.

Regus frowned at it. A dastardly thing of stiff fabrics and all these medals and titles he'd earned during the war plastered on one side. It was gaudy and too hot. He wished he didn't have to wear it at all. Ever.

Today was not his. Just as every day was not his. Today he was to do the queen's bidding. He was to marry a woman, a cousin of the queen, whom he had never met, and act as if he wanted a typical married life with his blushing bride for the following nights.

His eyes shot to his nightstand behind Doxy to the letter lying half torn where he'd left it. He received the answer to his last desperate plea to avoid marriage that morning. He would have to marry one Virsin Thesseolossos.

He turned, allowing the jacket to be shoved onto him, and then buttoned closed. Regus thought of a million ways to win a battle, to lead his men, and to intricately carve a path through enemy territory to kill the leader. This? How did one defeat the will of a queen and the norms of society?

"Doxy, are you sure you cannot think of a way to get me out of this?"

"Sir, once the marms and madams of the ladies get you in their claws, there is no escape."

He snorted. "I've killed hundreds-"

"Thousands. Millions, sir."

Regus' brow twitched, he had to remind himself the boy wasn't there. He hadn't seen the massacres. He didn't know what it meant to take a life on his own, not yet. "I have killed many," he waited to see if Doxy would point something else out, then continued, "But I cannot fathom how to escape a bunch of powdered women's desires toward me marrying one of their own?"

"It's a different type of battle, sir. One that no one knows how to win, not even the ladies themselves."

He watched as Doxy's gaze fell. The boy losing himself in his own thoughts that Regus hadn't an idiom of knowledge about. He stood patiently still as Doxy added the last finishing touches to his wardrobe. Frills and jewels, smoothness and sharpness, and Regus' own personal type of hell was upon him.

Perhaps the wedding would fall apart with an attack. Would he have that kind of luck? Probably not. They were in the capital and he personally made sure there was no danger here.

Steeling himself, he glanced at the man in the mirror. Scarred face with a more scarred body hidden behind peacock-like finery. Ridiculous. He sneered, the scar curling his lip in a grotesque way that usually washed witnesses of it in so much fear they shook in their boots. What would the little prim lady do if he turned that on her?

His snarl turned into a smirk. That was it. Scare the lady out of her wits and she'd run away. He didn't have to chase her, either.

He followed Doxy out of his chambers, adjusting the jacket one way, then returning it because it didn't feel any better at all. His armor wasn't as stiff as this damnable jacket. Tugging at the frilly thing at his throat, he growled, making the boy turn to look back at him with wide eyes. "Don't fix it until we get to the church," he told the boy, yanking the fabric loose around his neck as they made their way down the stairs and through the foyer.

He nodded at Mervas and Fince, his most trusted servants that ran the house in his stead, "We will return soon. Hopefully without a wife." He added the last under his breath.

Regus stopped on the threshold, looking out the door at his six. They too were in their finery, their handsomeness blinding even to him. His possible wife would probably take one look at any of them and run into their arms once he scared her. So be it.

Anything to not leave a woman destitute once he died was worth any scorn he'd receive.

He took one look at the ratty carriage and dreaded the moment he would have to ride in it. Not now. Now, he could be on his horse, and he did just that. Making quick work of the stairs, he took the reins from his second and mounted his stallion.

"Shall we stop for a last drink as a single man?" The redhead at his side asked with a smirk.

"We're already late!" Doxy cried at his other side.

Regus shook his head. "Let's get this all done and over with. I'll still be single after this day."

The redhead laughed heartily. "Dear Duke, you cannot go against the whims of the Queen. Not even you could survive that woman's wrath."

Regus swallowed, knowing it was true. After all, she'd brought his cousin, the king, to kneeling and performing her every whim. The woman was formidable, he had to admit, but he was sure he could get out of it and not be blamed.

It would all fall on the lady's wishes and desires. Who could deny a lady? No one should.

The ride to the capital was slower than usual, the rickety thing behind them doubling their time. He cursed himself for not having better time management with the painting and repairs of his finer carriages. Carriages gifted to him by his cousin, and he was sure it was because of the queen.

"Remember how to do the thing I taught you with your tongue?" The other redhead asked.

Regus noticed that Harry and Fedvich, who looked like brothers, flanked him; Harry was to his right and Fedvich to his left. He glanced at Fedvich. "You taught me many things with the tongue, and I remember them all."

"Good, use that tonight."

He rolled his eyes. "There won't be a tonight."

"Days and nights come and go, no matter what you wish." Slayth countered, "Make tonight count and plant your seed in that new wife so I can have a baby to spoil."

"Make your own," Regus growled at the elf, who rode somewhere behind him.

"The wife is of an age it would not be safe. Therefore, I must demand the second best, having you lot married off and giving me plenty of little baby cheeks to admire."

"Ah, but you must last, too. Don't spill until you absolutely can't hold back from taking her, but be gentle." Harry added, "Ladies like her have no experience. Untouched."

Regus ignored the rest of the commentary and instructions from his second and Fedvich. With each word they spoke, his determination grew to end the farce of marriage before it began. A pristine lady did not deserve to be saddled with the likes of him. What would happen to her if he were to marry her, sully her, and then die the next time a rebellion broke out? That wouldn't be fair to her. Not at all.

Reaching the capital, they rode through to the center where the church squatted, adorned in red swaths of cloth tangled in flowers. A priest stood at the bottom of the three steps leading to the wide-open double doors. Here it began.

"Sirs! You are late! You didn't get the chance to meet your new family, nor your bride! Go to the altar!" The priest's hands waved wildly, long sleeves flapping.

That would have been ideal, scaring the bride before the festivities even began with meeting her first. He cursed his luck as he dismounted and paused long enough for Doxy to do the same and fix his clothing. Regus strode into the church, his men filing in behind him and taking the empty benches on his side. He had no blood relatives other than the king and his offspring. His men were family enough.

The Seven were a family chosen by themselves.

He walked to the altar, noting the white and red dressed woman already there. She didn't turn. Her dress did little to hide the curves, and his mouth watered. Once he stopped at her side, he had every intention of performing his most nasty snarl, but his eyes caught on the beauty beneath the lace.

Fuck me...

Chapter 4
The Ceremony That Is Too Long

"Oh, my…" she said. She thought to herself, why do we have to do the ceremony? Can't we get into bed together already?

Her upbringing did not equip her for this. Her heart skipped beats while she imagined his appearance under all those wedding attire layers. It prepared Virsin Grym Thesseolossos for ladyhood. Duchess. Strict procedures in doing everything from waking up to how to hold a teacup, this era's women shared this experience.

What was she to do with the tall, broad, gorgeous, dark-haired man beside her with whom she actually wanted to perform some of those steamy scenes in the books she wasn't supposed to read?

Where had that lesson been?

Silence filled the church, and Virsin stared at her husband-to-be more until the priest cleared her throat. The new bride registered the sound enough to tear her longing gaze away from the profile of her husband. Observing the woman in red and white, she wondered what the woman's expression meant.

"Oh! I do." She had things she must do before she could be alone with her man, Duke Regus Brindle Norvasos, aka Duke Victory, in shining armor. Virsin's mouth watered as she imagined him in armor, sweaty, breathless, eyes hooded with hatred for their enemy. Then turning, in all his glorious self, to see her, and smile through the blood spatter.

What if he had dragon blood?! Oh, no, what if he was secretly an offspring of their enemy, fighting against his hateful family and she could help him trust and love again? What if at night, he changed into a voracious beast that only she could sate?

The last imagining made her weak in the knees.

"My lady," a rumbling voice thrilled her. He leaned in close to her ear through the veil, "Forgive me for tainting you in this way."

She stared at his large, calloused hands as they lifted her veil. Then his eyes caught her attention. Midnight blue, similar to staring into the night between sparkling stars before the sun fully relinquished the sky to the moon.

What was supposed to be happening? Right. A kiss!

She nearly jumped into his arms. But his hands were gentle on her sides. Virsin's gaze dropped to his lips. The bottom one was plumper than the top. From his jaw to the corner of his eye, a slender but ragged scar caused the left side to lift slightly.

She needed to lift her chin unusually high to see his face this close to hers. His strength, apparent under his clothes, nearly threw her imagination into another series of hopes and dreams. Until he came even closer, and his lips pressed to hers.

What was his tongue going to taste like?

Virsin blinked, staring at his lips because they were no longer on hers. The weak kiss was far too quick. Unclenching her hands from one another, she reached up. He turned, thwarting her attempted kiss.

She turned with him, the roar of the crowd suddenly filling her ears. Polite clapping still became thunderous when there were so many confined in a room that echoed like a cave. A unified salute, and a chorus of "Congratulations, lord," arose from the left rear.

She had never been so lost in thought or daydreams that she forgot her surroundings and the fact that she was not by herself.

He presented his thick arm. She wrapped her hand around the curve of his elbow. She was aware that walking down the lengthy purple rug to the entrance of the worship hall would be arduous. To each of his steps, she had to take two. Luckily for her, he shortened his stride after a few moments.

Considerate! He was considerate! How lucky was she?

What if he lacked the time and promptly brought her to bed? Should she complain about it or act shocked? Perhaps, instead, he seized her maidenhood within the carriage before reaching home.

She felt her face burn and tried to school her thoughts into place. *Concentrate on the here and now, Virsin,* she chided herself.

Her family glowed with grins and fake tears from their pews, and soon enough, they were behind the new couple. As they passed his men, she studied them. Instead of short cropped hair like the other regiments, theirs were long, kept neatly tucked into a black ribbon. How odd.

"My men wanted to be here to celebrate the occasion. I hope you don't mind their appearance. As soldiers, we are not smooth and kept like the gentlemen you are used to and probably prefer, my lady."

"I don't mind at all, and I do not have any preference over soldier or gentleman." Not anymore. "My preferences lie in actions and attitude, my lord." She reassured him with one of her winning smiles that half closed her eyelids but didn't show teeth. "Besides, I was only wondering why your regiment all have long hair, when the usual standard is short?"

"Very good, and I appreciate your candor." His smile was small and short-lived, "My lady, ours is long to provide warmth under our helms and a little more cushion. We were oft stationed in the colder portions of the battlefields due to our southern lineages."

He also explained things to her without disdain in his voice! She hoped he would catch her if she swooned in deference to her good luck. Gods, she would worship every day!

Instead of tossing her in the carriage as she'd imagined, he guided her to the side of the church where the celebrations building squatted. Decorated in white roses and red tulips, with similar hued cloths draped between and around the pillars, it was a beautiful sight to behold. They placed their seats on the raised dais behind a flower-adorned table covered in white cloth and plates of glistening or powdered delicacies.

Once he settled her in the chair, she found her favorite foods before her. Breaded pork cutlets drizzled in fried egg and a dark rich sauce, noodles cooked to perfection in mouthwatering herbs, and a red velvet cake with thick creamy icing made her salivate as much as her husband did. She glanced over to his side and noted his spread was much the same. But he also had a few more side dishes of grilled chicken in bite-sized pieces with some deep red sauce over them, and an oddly shaped breaded thing curled over another plate.

"My Lord and Lady, I am Count Rasmus and may I present to you my wife, Helena, and daughter Tarin. For your wedding day, we wish to gift you these jewels and a dagger made by our country's finest smith."

Her husband glanced at her, then he looked back at the family before them dressed in extravagant golds and blues as was their right as counts. "I thank you for the dagger, it looks like a fine weapon indeed. My lady, do you like them?"

She turned to stare at him, surprised that he was allowing her to speak instead of speaking for her, "Y-yes, of course I do. They are beautiful and I cannot wait to wear them. I pray I do them justice."

"You are very gracious, my lord. My lady." The trio bowed after servants took away their gifts and placed them in the side room on their left.

"I hope you do not mind me ordering most of the gifts to be packed away instead of presented. Here are a few I thought might interest you. Otherwise, your meal should be uninterrupted for you to enjoy fully." The duke spoke gently. His voice still grew in her ears and washed over her body, providing all sorts of sensations she didn't know a mere voice could perform.

"Thank you for being so considerate of me. I hope you enjoy your meal uninterrupted, too, my Lord Regus."

"Reg." He said quickly, "I am Reg to you, my lady."

"If I do, then you must call me Sin." She smiled at him.

His brows quirked, and his lips lifted, "Sin? My lady, I could do no such thing, for you are beauty and therefore cannot sin."

Oh, if he only knew the thoughts and feelings he caused in her. Hellfire was worth it for him. "I would not be so sure, Reg."

"But I am. If others name you Sin, I shall call you something special." He paused, picking up his wine chalice and swirling the contents as he thought. "I shall call you Beauty in public, Vers at home, and Sin only in our bedchambers."

This was sounding too promising. What was the catch? Oh, she didn't care. To hell with virtue, she would lose it all to him and surrender completely. "I enjoy nicknames." She answered with a smile. "Now eat, Reg. You must be famished."

Chapter 5
Only One Bench in the Carriage

He talked with her. Actually, *with* her and not *at* her. Every question she asked him was answered, and he asked questions of her and her family. Interest! It seemed he liked her well enough.

He was gorgeous and courteous to the extent that his skin could be spotted purple and she'd still beg for more.

"The night shall be used for travel, my lady. Forgive me this second discomfort to your constitution. My men wish to be home, and I cannot deny them any further." Regus spoke quietly, leaning closer to her as he offered his hand.

"It's no inconvenience. I would hate to keep them from their families more than they have already. The war was long for them." She took his hand, and he stood, pulling her up gently with him.

"First, I shall ask you to dance. Will you?" Regus' smiled to one side, his head canted to the other.

"Of course!" Virsin wanted to dance all night. Not really, but she needed to get this excess energy out somehow.

He led her to the middle of a small area between tables. The music changed, a waltz. His hand settled gently, but firmly on her ribs, and she placed hers in his outstretched one. She looked into his eyes and became captive. His lead was sure. Strength seemed to leak from him to her as he twirled them in the small space. He met her stare with his own. Virsin couldn't read a thing in the dark depths. Her instincts told her she had nothing to fear in his hands. Nor did she have to school her face into serenity, for his countenance was a welcome study.

She knew the dance was coming to a close, and she noticed something in his dark gaze spark.

He stepped off the allotted spot. Dancing them through the open walkway between the tables of his men and her family. She saw more than one grin from his comrades. Several fans and hands hid smiles on the women as their eyes crinkled and cheeks flushed.

The music stopped, and he released her side to spin her out to his. He guided her through the entryway, down the steps to the street, and into an awaiting carriage. It was smaller than she was accustomed to, and older. Her own weight made it squeak and unsettle in a rocking way.

When he climbed in, the area grew as cramped as their linen closet back home.

She scooted against the door as he settled himself beside her on the narrow, but comfortably cushioned bench. His shoulders ate up most of the room above, while his legs took the space below. Virsin was to fit against him, or fall out of the contraption.

She did not mind at all.

He tapped the roof, and they jolted forward, jostling them together. "Unfortunately, my finer carriages are being repainted. A miscalculation on my part. I hope this will not upset you." Regus said, turning in his seat to press his back against the side of the carriage to give her room.

"I bet the carriages will be glistening when they are done."

He chuckled, straightening his lapels, and drawing his legs away from her as best as he could.

"Please, don't concern yourself with space. We are married and…" Virsin began, but was interrupted by her new husband.

Regus cleared his throat. "That may be the case, but as we are just, I do not wish to crush myself upon you."

She felt disheartened. If she were as thin as the other ladies her age, he would have imposed on her already, she was sure of it. "You said you lived outside the city."

"Yes, on the other side. We shall be an hour in this dastardly contraption." Regus shook his head, "I should have asked to borrow one from Slayth, but I did not. I didn't think you would be so…" His inspection trailed over her face, resting on her lips, then back up to her eyes as he finished his thought, "Perfectly exceptional."

Was that a kind way to tell her she fell short of his expectations? She wasn't sure she should pry at the moment. What with his charming lopsided smile, beautiful eyes, and broad chest, she could not suffer his rejection in such a small space. "Who is Slayth?" Distraction was key to bar emotions from making her a fool.

"He is one of my men. He retired from being my second two years ago when I received this," Regus pointed to the scar along his cheek. "And the spear in my ribs." He then patted his right side. "Told me he was getting too old to protect me." He shook his head with a slight half chuckle.

"Is he?" Virsin asked, his face lit up when talking about his men and home. She wanted to keep the shine in his eyes.

"For his kind, no. For us, yes," Regus answered vaguely, looking over his shoulder out the window.

The sun's last rays lent a golden hue to the darkening sky along the craggy and rolling hill filled horizon. Virsin paused, watching the sunset, then questioned her need to constantly probe the man and her interest in Slayth. "Was it his fault?"

"Hm? Ah, no. Not at all." Regus shook his head, drawing his attention back to her as if she burned his gaze and he'd rather look at the sun. "My wounds are my own folly, not any of my men's."

"You have fought many battles for quite some time. Fifteen years since the war started, yes?" Virsin asked, trying to picture him four years ago, before the scar.

She probably would have fallen to her knees and begged for him if she had seen him scarless.

Not that the twist of his lips was severe. She didn't wholly mind it. Character. Yes, her husband's handsome face certainly held character.

"Twenty, my lady, twenty long years," his voice dropped as his gaze returned to the outside of the carriage. "Sleep, as I am sure you are tired. You may need it."

Promising, indeed.

Chapter 6
The Long-Awaited Night

She tsked, tossing the pin onto her vanity and staring at her reflection. "Drat it all. Up, out of the way or down so he can grab?" She had believed the current style would suffice and had sent her new maid away after the woman did a fine job of pinning her thick tresses up enough to entice further mussing. Now she was second guessing her choice.

It wasn't like she could call the maid back. Reg would enter at any moment. Her heart fluttered at the thought.

"Oh, stop." She waved her hands in front of her face as it turned from perfectly pale to red blotched in the mirror.

Throughout the celebration, she had planned what to wear of her lingerie. In the hours in the coach, she had tried not to drool over how he filled his seat in beside her, or how he shyly kept his gaze out the window instead of on her unless speaking to her.

A reserved, attractive warrior was about to walk into their shared bedchambers and reveal to her the essence of the most intimate connection between a man and a woman.

Virsin had many things to do.

First, the hair. She settled for it being half up and half down now.

Second, she needed the lighting to be perfect. Enough that she could study and touch his every scar, or muscle, but not so bright it would hinder their slumber after festivities. She wandered around the room, extinguishing one candle there and another here to create a romantic glow. At least she hoped it was romantic.

Third, her pose. Should she meet him at the door, and wriggle before him all shy like? Then he could pick her up and toss her on the bed with his brute strength?

No.

On the chaise lounge, she should pretend to read a book from the small round table. He would see where she was, how tumbled her hair appeared, but would have to come around to witness her in all her glory. Perhaps. She settled on the chaise, lying half up on the arm and curling her legs ever so slightly. This wasn't right. This furniture was far too small for him to do as he wished with her.

Virsin rose and padded over to her new sleeping arrangement. Looking at it, she tapped her finger against her bottom lip. Should she stay standing and lean back against the post? The one on the left, or the one on the right? Which side of the bed did he prefer?

Maybe she should lie at the foot across it. He could spot her from the door and she could watch lust fill his eyes. Virsin frowned, knowing that she fell short of the prim and proper perfection most of her kind were. Her hair was brown, bordering on black, and held waves instead of curls. She wasn't thin, but that helped with things most other ladies lacked until they bore children.

Already in possession of the boobs, ass, and thighs most of the men in the romance novels wanted, Virsin hoped he liked them, too. He called her beauty, so that had to be a sign he did. Virsin waved her hand in front of her face as she reimagined him saying her name, or nicknames, in this very room.

Crawling on the bed, she pulled at her lace nightie, settling it just right to cover over the important parts. She should not give too much away at first sight, right? She settled on one elbow, facing the door. Her other hand she slid under her breasts, pushing them up so they strained the lace just so. Perfect.

No. What if... she sat up, leaning on her hand and curving her back. This was better. It didn't seem like she was as desperate this way. Did it?

In the middle of scooting off the end of the bed to sit on the cushioned trunk there instead, a knock sounded.

"My lady, your lord husband has arrived."

Her mouth grew dry. She wasn't in a grand pose! He should wait!

But she wanted to welcome him. Would he be wearing a robe? Just pants? What did men wear for sleeping, actually? Did they showcase themselves with lingerie, too?

She planted her feet on the trunk, knees together and slightly tilted for chastity's sake, her hands on the edge of the bed to either side, pouted, and pushed her chest out, "You may enter, my lord."

The door opened just enough for him to step through, and he closed it behind him without looking her way. The turn he did seemed to stop time. But his midnight gaze finally landed on her.

She inwardly squealed as his lips parted and his eyes widened.

He was god incarnate. Had to be. Sun kissed brown hair framed his face and fell over his shoulders in waves to where his abdomen narrowed to his waist. That gaze of his was so dark, so deep. The scar on one cheek, showing his devotion to protecting his citizens.

Not a sign of scales nor bite marks to hint at a different lineage on his bare neck. Nor on the slim slice of tanned chest she saw between the lapels of his loose dark blue shirt. Another scar peeked at her from under the left lapel, though. So, she had a justification for touching there at least.

His pants were slack, too. Black. Perhaps they were loose enough to hide the bulge he should have. Or was he on the smaller side? Were romance books inaccurate concerning a man's erection while clothed?

What if... what if he was disgusted by her?

Nerves shot through her like ice spikes at the last thought. Her voice barely came out of her lips, "Reg?"

"You are divinity, my lady." His words were breathless, as if it used up all the air in his lungs to push them out.

Relief washed through her and comforted like a warm bath.

His strides were long, and she felt every breath she took catch with each one of his booted footfalls as he came closer to her. He was perfection. Lithe grace. A warrior lover.

He went down on a knee before her, "If I may?" His hand hovered over her bare left foot.

"Yes, please." *Touch me. Touch all of me. What are you waiting for?*

His hand was large over her appendage. The callouses rough, as he slid his palm around to cup her heel. He brought her foot up, just enough for him to lean down and kiss the top near her ankle. "My wife, you shall have nothing to fear from me. I will be as gentle and as kind as I may. I shall never touch you without your express permission." He smiled up at her, his eyes shining. "Your beauty will remain unblemished and intact for your next husband to enjoy."

It's starting! We're here! Finally, I get to see him naked! He's so gentle. What is he saying? Aw, that is so cute.

Wait.

What?

Chapter 7
I Made a Vow

"Sir, husband... why do you speak this way? I am your wife, and I am ready to serve you as your betrothed." Her breathing grew erratic. *What was he saying? Another husband? Was he a stand in?*

He sat beside her feet on the trunk, his hand still resting lightly on top of her foot. He gazed into her face, "I am thankful you are steadfast, and honor your duties, but you do not need to worry. I won't touch you." His lopsided smile did not reach the rest of his countenance. "I am not the worthiest of men, and my life is not my own. When the offer came to me, I tried to deny it, but her majesty the queen demanded we marry. I am sorry I could not convince her otherwise."

The queen, Lythaine. Her cousin. *Oh, beloved Lythie, you have gifted me a most precious gift indeed. Was this payment in helping her nab the king? It must be.*

He continued, "As my life is not my own, I cannot deny my worry over my touching you will injure your delicate sensibilities. The stress of being with me shall already cause harm to your constitution, I fear. To lessen the burden, I shall not bed you. I'll have extended absences, too. This way, you may live in peace." He patted her foot, "Get some rest, my beloved."

"Wha..." She swallowed, trying to get some words to come to her mouth by clearing out the dryness. "No, please. I am ready!" Virsin clutched his sleeve. "I have this on. We're married. I... we're sharing chambers!"

He squeezed her hand in reassurance, removing her fingers from his shirt, "These are your rooms. You may redecorate to your liking. Furnish the house as you wish. Have tea parties." Reg's voice was soft, with encouragement lighting his countenance. "Do things to make you happy, my love. I shall find you a fine replacement. Therefore, when I pass on, the transition will be natural."

"Why do you speak of dying so? You are young! Are you sick, Reg?" She touched his face, then brought her other hand up to the other cheek. He was so warm. His scruff prickled her fingers and palms.

"You are sweet to be concerned. Rest assured, I will meet my end on the battlefield, far from your presence. You don't have to worry about taking care of a sickly husband." He chuckled, straightening to flex his arms, and beat a fist on his chest, "Healthy and hardy."

Sexy and delicious. Ridiculous and kind. "My dear, the war is over, is it not?" She tried another tactic, scrambling to find convincing lines to feed him. Perhaps he truly did not like her appearance, and was saving her from disgrace and hurt feelings in this way? "If you dislike me, I may diet. I'll change."

His eyes flashed, and he clasped her hands in his as he put his face in hers, their noses nearly touching. "You shall do no such thing. Perfection cannot become more perfect. I will not have you harm yourself for some silly social rules. You are beauty, I shall tell you this many times until you believe me. I have a difficult time being here and not..." he paused, drawing back. "My base desires rise with every look you give me, your gentle touch, and the way your voice warms me."

"Yield to them!" She tried pulling her hands from his to grab him, but his hold did not give way.

He laughed, "My love, heed not your vows. You shouldn't strain yourself into doing such an act on my account." He shook his head, "You are adorable. I like this honorable streak you bare to me. If circumstances were different, I fear I should get nothing done for being unwilling to leave your side."

"It's no strain! I assure you. I mean... the first time might... I know little of these things, but I've heard that is-"

He interrupted her with his low rumbling voice, "Should be with one who is going to love and cherish you for the rest of your days, not for a short time."

"You will not die so soon!" Virsin trembled and pressed her lips tight for a moment to gather her wits. The perfect man she had dreamt of was now holding her hands, her husband, but he didn't want to fulfill her one wish? Some god somewhere was laughing cruelly.

"There is no longer hostility, my love. You shall live a long life with me." She smiled as sweet as honey, leaning forward. Excitement whipped through her when his gaze dropped, just as she had hoped. Then it fell as if he found interest in the rug at his feet.

"It is not known to the delicate. We have won the war, but there are still battles to fight. Resistance to squash. Even when signatures and seals are put to paper for evidence of peace, there are those we cannot control through words and ink." When he looked back at her, his gaze darkened in sorrow, and another pain she could not fathom.

"Then I shall make your life as wonderful as I can for as long as I have you with me!" Freeing her hand at last, she slid her fingers into his hair, reaching for the nape of his neck. His hair felt like silk bordered in cotton lace. Soft, but the ends and shorn areas were rough against her hands. Another scar slit through his scalp, creating a bare line of red she exposed in her hurry to get him to kiss her.

No, to kiss him.

She scooted to the edge, as fast as she could without falling, and leaned in as she tugged him closer. Closing her eyes, she tilted to fit to him. Feeling the warmth of his breath on her chin, she knew she was almost there.

Then his fingers closed over her wrist, his head twisted out of her grasp, and his lips brushed over her fingertips.

"My men have told me how devout some ladies are to attending their husbands after the wedding. I thought them silly, for of course their wives would be. Some of them are considered quite handsome." He squeezed her fingers gently before placing her hand back in her lap under his. "But now, I believe nobles are brainwashing their daughters into serving. How strange. It should make you angry, my love. This drive to serve me, for it is not truly what you want. This average visage bordering on horrid is not for you."

"I am angry! I'm angry my husband does not desire me! And on my wedding night, too." He called himself ugly? This man before her? "You are handsome." She stared at him as he did her. He blinked owlishly, before his brows drew low and together. A wrinkle appeared between them.

"I am greatly concerned for our ladies. For you, my beauty. You should hold yourself in higher regard." He nodded, as if setting something in stone, "I deign to find you a great husband indeed. He should be respectable, loving, and worship you."

"Why can't my current husband do that now?" Frustration licked through her, stoking her anger.

His face brightened, and brow smoothed. "Ah, indeed. What you are trying to say is clear to me now. I shall remain steadfast in telling you how beautiful you are. I will idolize you. Do not worry, my beauty. While one may call you Sin, I shan't allow you to be tarnished with mine." He stood, "Now then, get some rest. Sleep well."

Words would not pour forth, nor would they form in her mind for her to wrest them out. The same confident stride that propelled him to her earlier carried him away. Her heart dropped.

"What in the name of the gods is going on!" she cried once the door clicked shut behind him. Falling back onto the bed, she bit her finger to keep from screaming.

Springing up from her soft velvety bedspread, she paced before the four-poster bed. "I had everything ready for him!" She gazed down at herself, knowing she looked as good as she could.

"He's saving me for another man? He intends to find me another husband?" Sorrow filled her chest, and pricked behind her eyes, "He thinks he's going to die." She paced, contemplating, reviewing the conversation, and every word he'd uttered.

If he considered her beautiful, it was only a matter of time before she could convince him to show himself to her, to lay with her, and to romance her like in her novels. Right? She grinned, stopping in front of the bed with her hands on her hips, "Alright sheets, never fear, you will be broken in." Hopefully soon, she thought to herself.

Chapter 8
It's All So Deadly

The gentle glow of dawn colored the tree filled horizon. He stared at it, wondering how it was possible this day began like every other, except he possessed a wife. Damn the gods, he married the lady! What happened to his spur-of-the-moment plan of scaring her away from him? He had to come up with something.

Last night, his promises of not touching her were the best he could do.

All he could do.

Virsin was gorgeous. She was the most beautiful woman he'd ever laid eyes on. His chest hurt thinking about her, picturing her in his mind, and he ached for her everywhere else. Ached so much that he'd nearly given in to her last night. Taken her, tasted and felt her, like he desperately desired to. He'd never known a need like this before.

Did Fedvich train her to cause such desire in him?

He knew the man was actively still tutoring nobles and whoever could afford his services. Did Virsin's family take up his offer? Had the queen sent Fedvich to train her? That explained why she was so attractive to him and why he couldn't get her out of his mind.

That girl is poison, he thought to himself. A poison possibly created by one of his very own. It made her the deadliest weapon.

Speaking of weapons, he glanced at the glow limning the tree line. He needed to prepare for his first daily task. Training Doxy was the beginning of each day, as he couldn't take the boy into battle and toss him into it like he had the others. Each of them witnessed and felt the boy's potential and agreed he was to be their seventh member a little over a year ago. He needed to make sure Doxy Pomm was deserving of the distinction.

Regus strode over to his armoire and took out a handful of weapons, a few throwing daggers, a needle, a short sword, and a rock the size of his fist. The daggers he placed under his pillow. He positioned the smooth gray stone on a small shelf he'd made on the back of the full-length mirror Doxy demanded he be dressed at. The thin needle he placed on top of his nightstand, it would serve as a fine distraction from the daggers.

The sword he tucked in beside him once he crawled back into bed. The blade, cold against his bare thigh, was his favorite to use on Doxy this early in the morning. Somehow, Doxy hadn't figured out that this morning ritual they played was preparing him for battle.

The poor boy just figured Regus was not a morning person.

His mind drifted to the lady's chambers. While they were next door, sharing a bath, her sleeping chambers were two doors down the carpeted hallway. Was she still sleeping? Did she sleep in that lacy thing she wore? Was that an every night thing or had it been special?

Just for him, and he'd turned her down. Wasn't that more of an asshole move than keeping her for the man after him? No. No, it wasn't. It was worth it. This torture was worth it.

He didn't need to taste poison.

The boy's scuffling footsteps sounded just outside his door and he closed his eyes as he shoved his arm under the pillow to fit the throwing daggers in between his fingers. Regus deepened his breathing, adding a low rumble he hoped sounded like his natural snores. He bit back the grin as Doxy began shuffling back and forth in front of his door.

The poor boy was doing his best to gather up his bravery.

It was unfortunate that Regus shredded it each morning.

The door clicked, Regus flung two of the daggers, hearing them thud into the wood as he muttered sleepily and shifted on his bed.

"Fuck. Fuck. Fuck. I'm gonna die."

He sounded like a mouse, still at the door. Poor kid. Regus rolled, pulling his hand from under his pillow in a languid move that screamed of sleep before flicking his wrist to fling the last dagger at the boy. Damn, he was mooning the boy, but surely Doxy was used to his nudity by now.

"That was close!" Doxy's harsh whisper sounded breathless.

Did the boy catch it? Pride swelled in his chest. The boy was getting there. He would survive their next battle, or at least he had a fighting chance.

"Oh, please don't tell me he killed the duchess. Please don't tell me he ate her."

Since when had he begun eating other people in his fierce myths? He listened to Doxy's further begging whines to the gods about hoping he wouldn't find a dead lady in the chambers. He needed to remind Doxy that warriors often woke to things such as voices. Then again, it was easier for him to attack blindly if Doxy kept talking, too.

"Sir Regus, sir, time to... sir?"

He rolled his eyes, was that any way to wake a lord? He rolled back, hand gripping the hilt of the short sword as he flung out the other to land on the nightstand. The needle was gone.

"Good thing I moved that metal thing. Probably would have impaled his palm on it. Can't have that. He has to make the duchess happy with those hands from now on. Right? Yeah. That's what Fedvich said. I'm supposed to use lotion. Do we have lotion? Wait... that means I have to rub him... no. No lotion."

Regus couldn't help it. He chuckled and opened his eyes to regard the boy standing over him at the side of his bed. "No lotion? What if I'm sore from last night's activities?"

"But sir! I cannot- I- let the duchess do that as she's the reason you are sore!" Doxy sputtered and stammered, his face as crimson as a tomato. "Where is the duchess?" Doxy asked, looking at the bed as if the woman would spring up under the sheets.

"In her chambers, I imagine," Regus muttered, sitting up and pulling the short sword out to rest it across his thighs.

"You didn't eat her, did you?"

Regus eyed Doxy. His eyes were wide, intense. The boy was serious. "Since when do I eat women?"

"We are supposed to eat them in a way. Not in the way I'm thinking you did her. But you might have."

Doxy wasn't making any sense. While some of the Seven found it amusing, Regus was already bored with it for the moment. "Dox, let's get to training."

"Right!"

When the boy rushed toward the armoire and began pulling out his clothes, Regus stretched for the second time that day. What would she taste like? He shook his head, steering his mind away from such thoughts, for they would do him no service.

Also, Slayth was rubbing off on him. Doxy wasn't that much younger than he was, but he kept thinking of the young Pomm as a boy. Regus ran a hand over his face before getting up. He left the sword on his bed, Mervas would put it back up, and stood still as Doxy prepared him.

It was an odd feeling having someone dress you. He knew that as a child, a servant dressed him, and here he was again. Dukes were supposed to have several male servants. Regus had two, Doxy as his squire, and Mervas as his butler to take care of the house during his many absences. As soon as Doxy was battle hardened, he would be down to only Mervas again.

Was his new bride up getting dressed as well?

The thought of other hands on her made his blood heat. Why was that? What was wrong with him? It wasn't like he was going to touch her again.

He wanted to, and that realization caused him hate himself all the more. He hadn't a single claim to her. Forced into a marriage with a brute like him, she deserved far better than anything he could ever give her. Her rich curves and pretty little smile merited worship. His imagination made her face blotchy red with tears streaming down her rounded cheeks, and he knew he never wanted to see her cry. His resolved doubled. He would not touch her. Regus would find her a worthwhile man to praise her and marry her after he was gone. He would secure her future and safety.

He slid the needle from Doxy's pocket where he had left it and pressed the sharp end to the boy's chin. "You should always be aware of the dangers you are in."

"Well, to be fair, sir, you were lost in thought. I've been standing here finished for several minutes."

Regus' brow quirked, "You talk back now?"

As the boy spluttered and held his hands up, Regus chuckled. He handed the slender weapon to Doxy, "Put it up. You don't want to carry that around." He wasn't about to have Charn lose himself in the past because the boy kept the needle in his pocket.

Chapter 9
Divinity and Perfection Are Excuses

Late nights were her normal. It was well after the midnight bells tolled, she found slumber amidst her planning the loss of her virginity. It was around noon when she woke.

As she arose from her bed, the big thing swallowed her in coziness and large territory, she began her initial plan. First, dress. She had a penchant for showing off what she had, for it irritated the less endowed ladies so. Because of that, she had many tools at her disposal for her schemes.

The emerald green gown was soft to the touch, and the neckline plunged so dangerously low she always feared exposing the tops of her areolas. She rarely wore the thing for that reason, but today was not a day to be shy.

"Shall I add lace, my lady?"

"No!" she startled, then gave her best apologetic look to her annoyed maid, "Forgive me, Bea. No, thank you."

"But, my lady, you might... spill forth."

Virsin became amused at Bea's struggle to explain why she should have the lace. "Tis exactly why I don't want the embellishment, my dear. My husband shall have me in all my glory."

When Bea's slightly golden face turned as red as an apple, she knew she was on the right track.

"Do you think the duke likes hair up to show off a neck, or in a tumbled way?"

"I am not sure, my lady. I shall ask some of his other maids for his preferences if he has any if you wish?" Bea asked, watching her master in the vanity's mirror.

"Yes, please do. I want to know what kind of ladies he's entertained before, and if he's bedded them. If he did, what were their attributes? How did they dress? Of that variety." She should keep these notes and whatever she found worked on her husband. Although, Virsin hoped she wouldn't be in need of such knowledge gathering for long.

"My lady, do you really wish to know such things? Shouldn't your husband's past dalliances stay in secret?" Again, Bea's face was red, having no time to dim from her previous embarrassment.

Virsin pondered how to answer her maid without stirring up the wrong type of questions. As far as Bea knew, her husband had taken her like a man should on their wedding night. "Of course, that might be normal. But I want to impress him, keep him interested. I shall not bore him, for he is such a fine creature." Her own cheeks flushed.

"I see. I shall put your hair up in a way I think most men find interesting, then." Bea got to work, her thin hands quickly twisting and pinning her tresses into place.

It was a style similar to what she wore at her wedding. That should remind him of his vows, Virsin thought with a grin and thank you to her maid. Her makeup application was subtle, except for bolder lipstick. An intense red to draw his eye.

"Where is my husband?" She asked, giving her dress a twirl, pleased with her plan coming together.

As Bea shuffled through the papers detailing the duke's schedule and household things, Virsin tested how taking a deep breath would affect her neckline. And then bending over.

Perfect.

"He is on the training grounds. Would you like to take him a lunch?"

She giggled and twirled again, "Yes! Of course I should feed my husband."

When preparing, Virsin was not at all patient. It took too long for the cook to pack a picnic for them. Bea was lacking in speed when changing her slippers into boots as they waited on the lunch to finish. The kitchen's distance from the training grounds proved excessive.

She arrived, wine in hand, having given the basket to Bea halfway down the lane; the dress began working all too well before she had the chance to display its proclivities to her husband. She received the basket from Bea and took a few steadying breaths. "How is my hair?"

"Even better now, my lady," Bea answered readily.

"Good. If we go off somewhere, don't follow." She gave her maid a look, "And make sure no one disturbs us."

"Yes, my lady."

Granted, a blanket over the grass was a far cry from the comfort of a bed for her first time, but she would take it.

She listened to the clank of wood and some metal as she further gathered herself. Double checking her neckline, situating the basket and wine where neither would hinder the view her husband would gain by her entry, Virsin pushed open one side of the dark oak door set deep in the gray stone wall of the training grounds. Dust shimmered in the air in the bright sunlight. Sweat glistened on several hues of flesh ranging from pale to a rich black.

"Oh."

"Er... my lady, perhaps I should go gather your husband for y-"

"Nonsense." Virsin snapped, hating that Bea would try to take this view away from her so soon.

Men. Lines of them. Sets of them. Most in just pants, boots, and wide belts. They were glorious in their movements. It was as if she were watching several pairs dance to different types of music at the same time.

She didn't think training would be this beautiful.

Virsin vowed to take her lunch with her husband as often as possible.

Focusing on the task at hand, she scanned the crowd again, as not one of them seemed to notice her. Then she spotted a man with his hair color and followed the wild mass gathered on top of his head down to his face. The scar on the cheek was recognizable, but the ferocious grin was not.

"Oh, my..." She couldn't breathe. While all the other men were gloriously gorgeous, her husband surpassed them in beauty to her. He glistened like golden flakes upon a cloth in the sunlight. His skin, though imperfect, showed less scarring than expected.

The muscles.

She would hire a sculptor. An evil voice in the back of her mind chided, *At least then he would be hard enough to satisfy your lust.* That voice wasn't mistaken, but she refused to give in to rutting a statue.

A small stone lane ran down the length of the grounds, breaking the fighting pairs into two sides. She followed it to her husband and his sparring partner. They stepped out of the line of trainees, the strange knight now in full view.

Long red hair swung from a tie on the crown of his head, the ends split with tiny shining somethings. Crimson droplets melded with the sweat upon his back. When he jerked, his hair hit his flesh, causing more red to appear.

"My word! Sir!" she cried, rushing forward, "What is the meaning of this? Is this how you train your men, Lord Husband?!"

At her cry, the scuffling and clanging sounds stopped. All she could hear was panting, and her own footfalls, and whatever was rustling in the basket against her hip. She approached her husband and his sparring partner, concern filling her mind instead of her previous insidious plan. "He is being harmed with every step he takes! Stop this at once."

The large redhead threw back his head and began laughing.

Shocked, she stood still, staring at him. His beauty was indeed close to her husband's, but she preferred Reg. As she should.

"Ah, my lady, you are entirely too sweet for this beast." The redhead said, swiping at his eyes while sporting a huge grin and more than a few chuckles. He then cleared his throat, his heels snapped together, and he bowed with hand and hilt against his chest, "My lady, I am Viscount Harrick Tearney. If it pleases you, call me Harry."

"Sir, I shall take those things out of your hair, if you would just give me a moment." She shot a glare at her husband, who stood still by her side, sword point touching the ground between his boots. "What are you thinking, leaving these torture devices in?"

Harry chortled.

Reg sighed, "Lady wife, they are not torture devices in this aspect. Well, in a way." He shook his head. "They are used as training tools. No man should let adversity take him down."

"Or fall back, leaving his comrades at a disadvantage." Harry added with a wide, toothy grin. He tilted conspiratorially toward her, "To tell you the truth, my lady, you have fallen in with an odd crowd indeed. We enjoy a bit of pain." His brows waggled.

"Harry, I will have you refrain from making such comments to my wife." Reg stated, a bite to his tone.

"Oh, um… I didn't know… still!" She placed the hand holding the wine on her hip, tilting as she had seen her nursemaid do before scolding her, "It's dangerous, and painful. You should nurture yourself better!"

Harry's chuckle turned dark, "Perhaps the lady shall teach us how to take better care of ourselves, hm? She may mend our wounds and hearts each night after our long battles. Far better than old Tim, right?" He called the last out, looking over the men nearby.

They answered him as one, "Here, here!"

A voice, irritated, called back from the other side of the grounds, "My work's mending and cleaning, not holding you lot against my bosom."

"You have no bosoms!" Another man nearer to her cried.

The rest laughed.

Regus let them have their fun before holding up a hand, "Lunch!" He looked at her and said, "You shouldn't have gone to such trouble bringing me food. We have a kitchen."

Harry added, "Complete with burned pots for blackened fare."

"Don't you have somewhere to be?" Reg snapped, shooting Harry a glare.

"Yes, sir." Harry bowed with a chuckle and then blew Virsin a kiss, "My lady, I bid you farewell."

Chapter 10
Reasoning With Stubbornness Has No Reason

Virsin's next treat was to watch her husband wash from a bucket he drew up out of the well. Not having a free hand to fan herself was indeed a predicament. She thought these scenes in romance novels were absurd. They weren't. No. No, not at all. Every novel ought to include them on a regular basis.

The way his skin shone, and his pants clung to him...

Perhaps she could finally witness his length and girth if her plan worked.

"Shall we eat with the men, husband?"

He squeezed the water out of his long tresses, his gaze dropping to her chest, "No."

She bit back a smile, "Then where?"

He bound his hair up into a bunch of folds and twists with impatient fingers. Next, he grabbed his shirt and put it on, "Let me have the basket, my beauty."

She handed him the lunch, "You didn't need to get dressed on my account."

He chuckled, motioning for her to follow him, "I say even your sweetness would find the sight lacking after a while."

She frowned, staring at his backside as he led her out of the training grounds. Yes, wet pants were a luxurious view from this angle. "You lack confidence in your looks, and it confuses me."

"Why does it confuse you?" Eastward, he led her past the gray wall, extending a hand as they encountered a gentle slope.

She took his proffered hand and stepped carefully after him over the tumbling rocks and through the long grasses. "Because you are handsome."

His chuckle held too much amusement. "My love, you need not try to flatter me. As I told you last night, do not heed your vows. I don't require those lies." He paused, guiding her to the bottom of the hill, and then he stepped onto a dusty path breaking through the thick grasses. "I am not ugly, nor am I handsome. Your husband is average, would you not say if you were speaking the truth?"

"I speak truthfully when I state you are quite dashing, no, gorgeous, sir." How dare he question her. Did he think her a liar? "I do not lie! And I would not break that for your vanity alone."

She yelped as she smacked into his chest when he stopped and turned on her. How quick he was! Rethinking it, she stepped back into him, pressing her body against his. Delightfully rigid, and remaining damp.

"Perhaps I am of your favored preferences." He murmured, standing still in the light breeze stirring the surrounding grasses and distant tree boughs laden with leaves. "I know you are mine." He sighed as if she had broken his heart, "Thus my strength and vows shall be tested, for I shall keep you happy and pristine for the husband who will wed you next." He stepped away, turning to walk further down the path.

Virsin gritted her teeth, shaking the bottle of wine at his back. Lifting her dress, she trotted after him, "You are of my preference! If we had met in a ballroom, I would have swooned."

Another laugh.

She squeezed her skirts until her knuckles hurt, so focused on convincing him she paid little attention to their surroundings. "I would have!"

"Out of fear for the Duke of Viciousness?"

She paused, staring at his back, "The Duke Victory."

"Ah, that's right. A glorious word instead of the darkness peeking into noble houses." His voice was low, hinting at malice.

Shaking her head, she cleared it to keep on the trail of her plan. "Not fear. Overwhelmed by your handsomeness and how you fit my very dream of a man. Of a husband."

"Then your next one will keep you in a swoon state, I assure you, my love."

She wanted to stomp her foot like a toddler before a tantrum. Plan. Right. She reset herself, changing tactics and looking around him to the trail ahead. Not steep at all. Drat. She bit her bottom lip, trying to decide on which of the other two scenarios she could make play out.

Her boot slipped on a stone; she lurched forward, stumbling. Her teeth sank into her lower lip, enough to cause pain, and for the coppery tang of blood to touch her tongue. Regaining her balance, Virsin whimpered, touching her lip and looking at her fingertips to assess the damage.

Before she could do anything else, Reg had his hands hovering, "If I may?"

She nodded, staring into his eyes. The wrinkle between his brows was back.

He cupped her face in his palms, tilting her up. His thumb gently pulled her bottom lip down. So close.

A thrill coursed through her body, warmth spreading from him to tread in leaps and bounds all over.

"It's not too awful. Please be careful, my love." He crouched, opening the basket at their feet. After moving a few things, he pulled out a linen napkin. He stood, cupping her face again, touching her lip, and being so close she could almost taste him. Reg dabbed her wound with the cloth. "Yes, it is not bad at all." He smiled, his eyes raising to hers as he brushed his thumb away from her mouth to rest it on her cheek.

His look changed from concern to a light playfulness, complete with a small smile. "Since you do not find me completely repulsive, shall I carry you the rest of the way?"

"Yes!"

He snorted, and shook his head, "Well then, if you insist." He bent, scooping her up in his arms.

The spike of adrenaline when he moved so quickly and lifted her so easily made her squeal.

"Such an interesting sound." He murmured, tilting her down.

She scrambled for a hold, fearing he would drop her. His hot breath feathered over her bare skin close to her neckline, and she froze. This was perfect. Utter perfection.

She felt a bump against her behind and frowned. The basket, not a thing to get excited nor hopeful about. "Are you sure I am not too heavy?" She hoped she hadn't hit him with the wine bottle in her madness to clutch him.

"I shall ignore the question; since you overlooked my remark regarding your cute piglet-like sound.

"I do not sound like a piglet!"

"Ah, perhaps not. Chipmunk then?"

His playfulness made her breath hitch, and she jutted her chin out and straightened her back. "It better be a charming chipmunk."

"It is. Cute even when it is indignant over some pretend insult."

"This creature sounds very human. Is it your companion? Do you handle it and play with it often?" She kept her gaze on his profile, delighted when a red tinge creeped over the shell of his ears.

"I wouldn't say it is a pet, and I do not touch it." His voice dropped. He looked down, carefully picking his way over the rocky trail. "We will arrive soon."

"Pets and things you are vowed to should be handled often. Or they may fear they are not loved." She struggled to keep hinting instead of saying what she meant. "And if played with consistently, they will be happier. Happiest."

More red entered his ears and spread to tinge his cheeks as well. "Is that so?"

"Yes, my lord husband." Was he considering it? When they got to wherever they were going, was he to finally become her lord and master?

"Very well, I shall make sure to give my little chipmunk several pats on the head."

She frowned; suddenly not convinced she made her point at all.

"We're here. What do you think?"

So focused on the conversation and the way his body felt against hers, she hadn't paid a single bit of attention to their surroundings. He could have walked into a dragon's cave for all she knew. It wasn't a cavern, not at all. Before her was a bubbling creek with white sand beaches and large trees leaning over the water to lend shade. Sunlight dappled along the ground, birds sang in the thick branches, and frogs joined them in harmony.

"It's beautiful."

His smile was grand. "I expected you would like it. If you want, I will purchase a small table and chairs to put here for your pleasure."

"That would be nice. You will have to bring me here many times, then." His thoughtfulness warmed her, and she hoped she could show how much she appreciated him.

"I intend to when I'm able," he said, leaning down and placing the basket on the ground before settling her on her feet. "Perhaps, when you remarry, you can show your husband this, too."

Chapter 11
What Did You Do, My Lady?

"I'll have you understand, I carried this to you intending to convince you I don't want another husband. You are my husband." Virsin said as matter-of-factly as she could. She walked around the basket so she was facing him when she bent to open it.

She pulled the blanket out and barely heard him utter a sound in his throat. Smirking to herself, she unfolded it and spread it on the sands. She knelt, then went down on her hands and knees, smoothing the fabric in wide slow sweeps.

"Virsin, allow me. You are... you are exposed, my love." His gaze averted as he took the opposite edge from her and tugged it smooth. He was as far from her as he could manage without running across the stream.

She giggled, "Darling, you're the one who brought me out here. If you feared me being in the wild, or exposed as you say, then we should have picked an area closer to home."

Virsin watched his eyes fly to her chest, his face flooded with red, and he licked his lips as if he was about to taste her. At least his mind was finally in the correct spot. She sat back on her heels, spine straight, hands folded in her lap, and looked at him curiously. "My love, are you alright? You're flushed." She leaned forward again, reaching for him, trying for her most concerned expression.

"No. My lady, p-please." He motioned to her chest, his fingertips nearly brushing her arm, and he pulled away as if stung.

"Was there a bee?" She glanced around, in all the wrong places, before looking back at him. "I do worry about you, Reg.

You are practically feverish in your demeanor." She crawled forward, stopping when he rolled back on his heels.

"No. No, no bee." He stammered before swallowing heavily, his gaze jumping between her face and chest like a ball bouncing along the stairs. "My darling, you are indeed exposed. You sh-"

"Oh nonsense. It's just us here." She sat back again, tugging the sandwiches and plates out of the basket. Each movement a measured tactic to lure his eyes where she wanted them. "A husband and wife. Alone. Nice soft sand and blanket."

"Virsin!" He huffed, covering his face with a hand, "You have a breast out."

Frowning, she forgot herself for a moment, then she gasped and looked down at her chest. "Reg! You mischievous man. No wonder you were practically feverish!" She giggled, covering her breasts with one hand while the other covered her mouth. "If you wanted a glimpse, you should have peeked last night, you rascal."

"I-I-I- you fathom why I left you to rest. You were weary. Another husband." He struggled with words this day as she had last night.

"I was not tired, and I want no other man. I long for you." Surely, he would feel the truth in them.

His midnight eyes shot to hers, wide and wild. "You not know of what you speak. No. You know not... I cannot. The man I choose as my replacement merits this. Enough respect to keep you for him. Yes." His jaw muscles worked tight, and fists sporting white knuckles clenched on his thighs.

Was he trying to convince her, or himself? Her grin stopped short with the pull of her lip. At least she hadn't given him a hint she was stringing him along. Virsin pressed her breast into her dress as she tugged the neckline enough to let it settle back correctly.

"All is well now, lord husband. Your thoughts may remain chaste." She watched him crack one eye open. It's possible she should have undressed. His unease led her to the conclusion that his willpower was dangling by a tight, thin thread. Perhaps, with another few pushes, she could have her way with him.

What should she do to him first? Kiss him all over? The male figures in the stories appeared to have a special fondness for receiving kisses on their manhood from their women. That should be the initial thing. Would it hurt her lip? She cursed herself for her clumsiness.

Unwrapping the sandwiches, she scooted close to him as soon as he settled down. He was on the edge of the blanket; still as far away from her as he could manage. She changed the dynamic quickly enough. "Here, my husband."

She held the sandwich up to his chin, making her countenance innocent with wideness and openness, and her lips curled into a kind smile. "Food tastes better when it is from the fingers of someone you love, don't you think?"

"It's been said that food is more enjoyable when prepared by another. I realize deliciousness depends on the cook. But I'm unfamiliar with this... feeding a love thing." He spoke with a wariness to his tone, his eyes staying strictly on the sandwich in her hand.

"Let's try it. Say 'ah' my love." She made her mouth into a little 'oh' because it's what the women in the novels did to drive their men crazy.

He did, then took a bite of the sandwich when she put it close. Watching his mouth this close, and his tongue slip out to lick his lips, made her tremble. *What was that about, dear body?*

She handed him a half and said 'ah' for him.

She bit into it, messily, and felt the plop of the creamy cucumber salad against her cleavage. Perfection. After licking her lips, she blushed once more imagining the sounds he would make at night. "Oops." She put his half of the sandwich down, cupped her breasts and pushed them up as she bent her head. She lapped at the spillage.

The sound he made had her jerking up to look at him. His eyes were darker, mouth parted, his lungs working more as his chest rose and fell in great lengths. Then he was on his feet, grabbing the two halves of a sandwich they hadn't touched yet and shoving one into his mouth.

"Wha..."

He was a whirlwind of motion, throwing the dishes and napkins in the basket, along with the bottle of wine. "I need to return to the training grounds. My men are calling for me. Thank you for lunch."

Deserted, she stared up the trail. Never had she witnessed a man flee from her so swiftly in her entire life. Should she be concerned? Should she count that as a step in the right direction? Or the wrong one?

She stood, finishing the last bit of the half-eaten sandwich in her hand while watching the water flow by in its giggly way. Contemplating her husband, she sighed. What she knew for sure was the dress worked. She'd stirred him. However, she wondered whether he was moved by attraction and lust, or by disgust and hatred.

He could've at least left the wine. Part of her plan had been to get partially intoxicated, so he had to handle her. But now, as she thought about it, tipsy would not have helped her. He was too honorable.

"Drat." She brushed her hands off, letting the crumbs fall by the stream. She picked up the blanket and folded it before beginning her trek back up the trail.

It took her longer than it had with them going down. Of course, he had carried her for half of it. His stamina was wondrous! If only she could get him to use it in the correct ways. For her. At night.

The clanging and yells from the training grounds seemed more rigorous and taxing. As she passed the doors, both wide open, she peeked inside. She imagined this was what a battlefield resembled. Half the men lay collapsed; few leaned on swords; and still others looked up at the sky, as if praying. Several circled a central figure; recognizing him, she knew it was an incensed Regus.

"My lady, may I suggest something?"

She jumped, clutching the blanket to her chest and looking up into the almond brown orbs of Harry who leaned crookedly against the wall next to the door. "Y-yes?"

"Next time, ride him until he's tired so we won't get the brunt of his frustration."

Her face was on fire, "I-I-I." She stomped her foot, "Believe me, I want to!"

Harry's eyes grew wide, "Excuse me, my lady?" He breathed raggedly, and bruises covered his upper arms and shoulders. "What do you mean?"

"He refuses to touch me." She choked on the words, pulling the blanket up to her chin as she spoke.

Harry recoiled, tilting his head. He looked her up and down, "Surely you jest! My lady, that is a fine joke!" The redhead laughed heartily, slapping a hand on his flat stomach.

Before she could correct him, a thunderous voice drew their attention. "If you have the strength to laugh, you have stamina to fight. Get in here, Harry."

"Ah fuck me." Harry muttered, taking his leaning sword from the wall beside her. "But please, do us the favor of doing as I suggested. My lady," he bowed, and trotted to the center to help his lord ward off the rest of their companions for two hits, before he turned on Reg to aid the men.

Chapter 12
If I May Make a Suggestion

"Gods Reg, I can't feel my legs." Harry cried, "You've made me immobile!"

Regus rolled his eyes, staring up at the bright blue sky. Gone were the tremors of need coursing through him. He was content. The beast within sated with the excessive exercise. His seven lay in a circle, their heads toward the center. If they stretched their arms out, they might be able to hold hands.

The idea amused him enough that he studied the redhead beside him, then thought better of it. Harry was not in the mood. While he was joking on the outside, he could tell his second did not want to be touched, nor teased. He turned his gaze back to the sky.

"Boy, what happened?"

"His gorgeous wife teased him." Harry answered for him.

It wasn't completely truthful, but sufficiently close for Regus to allow the boys to believe it.

"Does it mean I'm going to get a baby soon?"

"Gods, I hope not, we have enough trouble with the sixteen you've had." Harry muttered. He then turned his head, "So?"

Regus could see and feel the curiosity on Harry's face, even if he didn't turn toward him. This would not be easy. He had to keep his wife pristine, but his men wouldn't understand. They were whores, the entire lot of them. Other than Bertran. The old man was his only island of solace in this mess. Why did he marry her? How did she trick him into saying yes on that altar instead of scaring her away?

She felt so soft. Everything he'd touched on her was soft and warm. Her lips, her hands, her ankle, and gods, he wanted to know what her warmth felt like seeping through the thin little lace thing she wore. That would sate their curiosity. "She's warm."

"I'd hope so. She doesn't look like a corpse." Harry spat back, "Dammit man, next time she comes on to ya, just take her. I can't survive these kinds of beatings because your dick is hard."

Charn piped up, "I volunteer Fedvich's ass as relief next time."

"Oh, fuck you. He's rough when he's pent up." Fedvich cried directly across from him.

"You're used to not being able to sit for a week from a good dicking. I'm not used to being beaten." Charn added, "The last time I was knocked down was from you riling him up until he had to burn off the excess."

"You owe us." Slayth chuckled.

"Fuck. No. Next time I see her carrying a little basket, I'm going to send her right back," Fedvich said.

Regus steadied his breathing, his own panting annoying him. "It appears we need new training to remind them of how weak they used to be."

"Yes!" Bertran bellowed.

"Gods! No! Anything! I'll die!" The cries sounded all at once from various members of his seven. It was odd calling them Seven for he was part of them, too. After all, they were the elite, and he had to be willing to be tamed for them to have a chance against him.

Virsin needed a chance, too. She was part of him now. Only Slayth was married. Perhaps he could have them protect Virsin when he was gone. He frowned, negating that. If he were gone, more than likely they would follow as they protected one another till death.

"Virsin is to be protected by all means necessary." He said, not raising his voice to cover the din from the men arguing against Bertran's training. He listened as they quieted, watching a bird fly across his line of vision high in the sky. "She deserves better."

Harry snorted as he said, "Well, that's an understatement. Just promise me you won't fuck her as hard as you did Fedvich that one time and we won't have anything to worry about. She's safe."

"I mean, if she likes it that rough, go for it. But not until she gets used to actual sex." Fedvich added, "The first few times are rough for ladies with gentle sensibilities and less knowledge than rabbits on intercourse."

That brought up the other question. Regus turned, lying on his stomach to look across the circle at the top of Fedvich's head. "Did you train her?"

He watched as Fedvich arched, looking at him upside down, "No. Why? Is she good? Maybe I have competition in the area."

Regus shook his head, "I..." He wasn't sure he should say anything, but he had to sate his curiosity, "The moment I saw her I wanted her. All the plans and denials left me and I said yes to marrying her. I had every intention of saying no. Scaring her. What was that?"

Slayth began cackling, "Oh, my boy, that is what you call love at first sight. It happens. Rare. It's only happened to me once out of the four wives, but you are struck with her on a level both basic and complex. Enjoy it."

That didn't help matters. He studied Fedvich, who looked as thoughtful on the subject as he should be. Was it love at first sight? He snorted, rolling to return to his back. He found himself smitten. Fascination. That's all it was. Once he found her a new husband, it would go away.

"Does that happen?" Harry asked.

Fedvich said, "I deal in lust, not love. I'll take the word of the old elf, though."

Doxy chimed in, still sounding as if he hadn't caught his breath, "It happens! My parents were that way, or they say they were."

"It wasn't arranged?" Fedvich asked.

"No. They married for love," Doxy claimed.

"Hm, that's something to remember for future reference." Fedvich said under his breath.

Regus shook his head, knowing the boy wouldn't know what Fedvich meant by his words. It was odd, Fedvich interested in one and acting the fool. He'd never seen the man flounder so much.

There was a first for everything. Love at first sight. Ridiculous, but it explained a few things.

Chapter 13
Obviously Not So Obvious

She was in her room. Pacing. She hoped this would not become a regular occurrence in her new house. In an hour, she was to take a tour of the residence. She had time to reflect.

Harry obviously considered her pretty enough to...

Her face burned. How had he put it? Ride? Yes, she remembered two or more of the romance books calling sex a ride or riding.

Harry was one man. Her husband was another. What Harry found attractive could be horrendous to Reg. Right?

She bit her bottom lip, then cursed as it pained her. Even eating the sandwiches earlier had hurt. Virsin recalled the scars on the warriors at the training grounds. She couldn't imagine their pain. A bit lip was nothing compared to that.

She pulled her shoulders back. "I will ride my husband. I will take care of him. His men will feel the respect and love I have for them as the wife of their lord." She nodded at herself in the mirror.

Virsin reviewed the steps which remained of her plan for the day. Put on a normal frock. Take the tour. Ensure the servants knew she loved the house and its master, and she would do her best for them. Change back into the green dress for dinner with her husband. Find a way to get into his arms, even if she had to pretend to be clumsy. Perhaps she should go further and make sure his face landed in her cleavage.

Yes, a sound approach.

Her gorgeous spouse. The idea of him touching her made her flush and tremble. His smile, his voice, his strength. He was everything. She couldn't so much as daydream about her favorite male leads anymore. They paled compared to him.

She had it bad.

Smacking her cheeks with her hands, she stared at her reflection in the vanity, willing her naughty thoughts away. "Very well, Virsin. Let's prepare for the second challenge of the day, shall we?"

As soon as she called Bea in, they set to work. She changed into her favorite blue dress for the tour; the emerald gown was spot wiped clean. They chose the jewels, and her necklace should help her stand out and draw his gaze. They prepared just in case the exploration went on a little longer than expected.

It was time for the perusal of her grounds, and she skipped down the hall, happy with her plan. In the foyer she met the head maid, Fince, and butler, Mervas, and followed them around. Listening intently as they detailed the architecture, and named off the faces in the few portraits. The kitchen was lovely. She always adored kitchens for their smells and bustling about. The drawing room used for greeting guests could use a few touch ups here and there. Some furnishings appeared worn. She could easily purchase some fabric and reupholster them.

The other drawing rooms she didn't worry about, not yet. They were for her utilization, or for the servants to do paperwork or take some lessons in. She commended the butler and head maid for ensuring their staff received an education. Few nobles would spare the expense of doing so.

"It was Lord Regus' idea, my lady. He desires preparedness for unforeseen circumstances."

Virsin opened her mouth to ask, but then thought better of it.

"Is there something you wish to say, my lady?" The head maid asked.

No need to be shy, was there? "I was wondering... is his lordship sick? Why does he speak as if he is about to die in his next breath? Has he always been that way?"

Fince looked at Mervas, as if speaking silently with one another.

"My lady, it is not that he is unwell," Mervas clarified, adjusting his tie as he spoke. "It is... well... ever since the war began, he's spoken and prepared for his death. He thinks it inevitable."

"Then… then shouldn't he worry about providing an heir to the estate?" Virsin asked quietly, not sure if she should bring it up or not.

The two shared another look. Fince answered this time, "He fears a child being attached to him will hurt the young one when he passes. The heir is you, my lady, and whomever you marry after my lord's passing."

Regus considered everything for others. Even if it was in such a ridiculous way. She wondered if he ever thought about his own wants and needs. Virsin was determined to find out.

Back in the emerald dress, hair piled up and curled until it tumbled messily about, she made her way to the dining room. It was beginning to be her favored style.

She paused in the hall, a few doors away from the food. The amount of chuckles and clinking disarmed her. Were they not having dinner alone?

Virsin debated changing, but threw the idea out. If he wouldn't act on his own, perhaps Scheme E would work best. The plan with jealousy in play.

Striding the remainder of the way down the passageway, she entered the open dining room, sweeping her gaze over the men. Of course, they were now washed, groomed, and dressed. She smiled as Harry made eye contact with her.

"Ah, there is the lady of the house!" Harry raised his glass to her.

"Here here!" The rest of the men cried, slapping their palms on the table with each word.

Reg rose from his place at the head and strode to the vacant seat at the end. He pulled it out, "Lady wife."

"Thank you, Lord husband." She said, concerned when his eyes never sought hers. Once she was settled, he stood behind her chair for a moment.

"These are my most trusted men. They call themselves something absur-"

"The Seven Vicious Tamers!" They cried in unison with equally wide grins.

"Right. As I said, ridiculous."

She noticed him signaling rightward out of the corner of her eye.

"This is Bertran, third in command." Bertran bowed his head, the loose salt and pepper strands flowing forward off his shoulders to hide his sharp, weathered features. "Next to him is Fedvick," another redhead, "then you have met Harry, my second." Harry gave her a conspiratory wink and grin. "To the right of my chair is Charn," A slight lift of his chin had her question his rank. "Slayth," was the name of the other wisened gentleman present. "And this one next to you is my squire, in a way, Doxy," who promptly bent his golden head low enough he nearly hit the table with his forehead.

Reg strode back to his chair as he said, "These men usually dine together with me. If they are too much trouble, I shall send your meals to your room so you may eat in peace if you wish."

"Now, see here, Vicious. You are supposed to offer to kick us out!" Slayth shook his head solemnly. "What is a dinner with your beautiful wife compared to stinking men?"

"I bathed! Did you bathe?" Harry cried, then turned to ask Fedvick with a loud sniff in his direction. "Ah, I see what he means."

Fedvick smacked Harry on the rear of the head, then winced, "Don't you ever take those whip tips out?" He shook his hand after studying it.

"Look, if you want to fight, you may ask. Don't just smack me and dig the little pricks into my skull." Harry bemoaned as he stroked his scalp.

"You liked it," Charn piped up, his voice lighter in tone than it should be. "Sadist."

"Masochist, get your terms correct if you're going to start calling names." Slayth glared at Charn.

"Yes, it's our fearless lord who is a sadist. Torturing his poor wife by not filling her enough." Harry leaned forward, grinning wickedly while wiping little droplets of blood onto his napkin.

"What?" Slayth looked from Virsin to Reg, back again, and then to Harry.

The redheaded masochist lifted a shoulder, holding the deadly glare of his lord, "I heard it from the lady herself. I thought it a joke, but considering the beating he gave us this afternoon... I doubt it was."

Bertran leaned toward her, his demeanor solemn, "Our dear lady, are you safe? Satisfied? Does our Vicious torture you? We will protect you."

Her face flamed, "I hardly know what to say."

"Say nothing." Reg warned.

"Oh no, please tell us details." Harry chimed back in.

She swallowed, looking down at her hands in her lap, "Well, we haven't... I haven't been able to fulfill my duties as a wife in the bedchamber."

Chapter 14
Called Out to Dig In

Amid the shocked grumbles were the chortles of Harry and Slayth demanding answers.

If her husband's eyes could kill, Harry would have been slain by Reg sometime last month.

"Quiet." Reg's voice whipped out, and the room silenced immediately. Servants poured in, carrying the first course. Once the doors closed behind the last one, the lord continued speaking, his gaze shifting to the end of the table. "I have explained myself."

"Then explain it to us!" Slayth cried, "I was hoping you'd tell us a little boy or girl would join us on hunts or I could babysit soon!"

His words warmed her heart. She could imagine a dark-haired, big blue-eyed boy on Slayth's shoulders, giggling.

"Eat." The command whipped out much like the word to silence them did.

"I shall waste this food if you do not explain yourself, my lord." Bertran leaned back in his chair, his stormy eyes trained on his lord.

"Same!" Doxy piped up, then slunk deeper into his seat as Reg glared at him.

Regus' nostrils flared, then he returned his gaze to Virsin. "I could die in battle at any moment. Tis unfair to my lady, my wife. For she is beautiful and kind. For this, I am respecting her next husband, whom I hope to find and arrange soon, in case of my death."

"Gods." Harry snorted, putting his spoon back down in his half-eaten soup. "You are dense."

Reg must have kicked him under the table, because he jerked and hissed in a breath through his teeth.

"I've told him he is my beloved and I want him as my husband. Is his death truly so inevitable?" Virsin twisted her napkin in her hands by her bowl while lowering her lashes.

"Of course not!"

"He's young!"

"He's an idiot."

All rang out at the same time, along with soothing croons from Bertran as he rested his large, rough hand on top of hers.

Reg's mouth worked, his lips twisting and then pressing as his narrowed eyes stayed on his wife. "Anything else you wish to arm them with, my love?"

Guilt? No. Shame? Hardly. What was this feeling? Triumph. Yes.

She tilted her chin, thinking of the worst things imaginable, so tears heated her face, "I want to fulfill my duties and make you happy, my lord husband. I am not arming them."

Fedvich leaned close to Bertran, "She's good." He whispered, and he gave her an appreciative smile.

"Yes, she is. Wonderful show, my lady. You'll have him in place in no time." Bertran nodded as he spoke low.

How did they know she was acting so quickly? Virsin wasn't sure if she should feign innocence with these two, or not. She smiled a little, lifting a shoulder slightly.

"It's viable. She deserves to be treated well, worshiped, and kept pure for her next wedding. I have no right to claim her body." Reg's words tumbled down the table to her as he tried to explain further.

"That's like keeping a slice of cake for a bad day. You keep putting it off because you're sure there are going to be worse days. You never decide to eat it. Then when you finally do, it's spoiled and repulsive. Do you want her to get moldy and gross?" Doxy asked vehemently.

Harry chuckled, "Dear Doxy, women don't get moldy. They get even." He turned back to Reg, "Do you want to keep her pure until the day she falls in love with someone else, and yet you have survived this war? What then? Will you still give her up, or force her to choose?"

"Or," Slayth added with a finger up in the air, "You die and she's tormented by not having a child to remember you by."

"What is it with you and kids?" Fedvich asked with his brows together.

"They are what we should be. Happy and free." Slayth murmured.

Reg picked up his bowl and drank from it as if it were a glass. He set it back down on the table with a clash against its plate. "I didn't know my private life was a topic of discussion among my men."

Most of them laughed, and Bertran retorted, "Sir, your personal life isn't secret to us. Neither is ours to you."

"Truth. We know everything about every single scar, the first time your cried like a baby into your pillow-"

"And the last one." Harry added to Fedvich's speech.

"Right." Fedvich agreed, "And we can give you tips on how to satisfy your wife if that's what you're afraid of."

"Gods know your equipment is fine." Doxy muttered under his breath. When the men looked at him, he held up his hands, "How many times have I dressed him?!"

Slayth cleared his throat and faced Reg, "I've been married for... years, sir, and I can readily give you any advice. It might work, it may not."

Virsin considered each comment, storing them for later use. This was a wonderful experience. She loved these men! Eagerly taking her side and making Regus see how foolish he was being.

His equipment was fine. Her mouth watered. Would she be able to evaluate for herself tonight?

The servants entered, removing the soup and presenting the next course.

The yeasty bread wrapped around ground meat and finely sliced vegetables smelled as delightful as it looked. The men in the room were quiet as they quickly finished it. It must be good, Virsin thought, if they stilled the conversation for it.

She took a nibble. Closed her eyes and whimpered. With another bite, she lost all sense.

"My lady wife," Reg's voice broke into her heavenly experience. "I am particularly glad you enjoy this course."

"For sure." Harry grinned at her, then leaned toward Reg, "Imagine, sir, the sounds she'd make for you, hm?"

With a clatter, Harry dropped to the floor amid his splintered chair legs.

"What does that come to, eight chairs now?" Bertran asked.

"Six under Harry, one under Slayth, and another with Doxy. This makes nine." Charn counted, touching his thumb to his fingers on each.

Virsin felt excitement march alongside wonder. Her husband had broken an oak leg so easily. And quick, too.

Harry rolled to a standing position, bouncing on his toes once before brushing himself off. "Maybe if you'd partake, you wouldn't be so prone to solve everything with violence!" He ducked as soon as he finished the sentence. The butter knife twanged into the wall behind him.

He had a good aim. What else was he skilled at? Virsin wanted to ask a million questions and hear all the stories.

"Says the monster who bloodies himself for pleasure." Reg snapped out.

"Oh, please partake. The war is ending. Your funds won't be able to hold with you, breaking everything under every person you don't agree with." Fedvich sighed heavily with a roll of his eyes to the ceiling.

"My finances are fine." Reg said with clipped words.

Silence fell as servants cleared debris and served the next course. Mervas placed a new chair for Harry, and with a bow said, "Sirs, enjoy your meal without killing one another. I thank you kindly." With that, he turned, pulled the knife out of the wall with a grunt, and left.

"I am honestly surprised none of us have killed Harry yet," Slayth said, rubbing his chin.

Chapter 15
Hopes and Dreams

Her husband told her to go to bed ahead of him. He had a few things to discuss with his men about tomorrow's training. Hope welled within her, and she let the giddiness soar.

She thanked the gods for The Seven Vicious Tamers.

Virsin ruminated on why they called him Vicious, while everyone in the capital knew him as Victory while laying out her lingerie. Bea stood beside the bed, ready to fold back up any she chose against.

Red might be a bit excessive, considering how much Harry annoyed him at dinner, Virsin thought as she pointed to the red slip and loincloth.

Blue would pay homage to his irises, but she had nothing dark enough. Would white be... ridiculous? No. She motioned for Bea to put up everything but the white pieces.

The wrap and breast strap might be too much. She took it away, not wanting to appear too desperate. Next, she studied the long silk garment cut like a low neckline gown at the top, but slim against her thighs and down to her knees. She liked it, but would he?

The other choice was an under-bust with lace to go over her chest. That was it. Similar to the loincloth, she was sure it would be too much. Bea helped her out of her emerald dress and into the nightgown. Brushing her hair into a shine, and washing her face to remove the day and make-up, Bea then left after turning down the bed.

She couldn't very well remind him of their last night. Virsin avoided posing on the bedding and opted to sit on the chaise until she heard his knock. Then she would welcome him in, standing. Yes, that would be best. Eager to see him, but not desperate. Right?

If he was discussing tomorrow's training plans, did it mean he wanted to sleep in with her? Her cheeks flamed again, and she held her face with her cool hands. She had read in many of the romances that men pleasured their women for hours, way into the morning. Would that be the case tonight?

Maybe they could talk of their future together and not have him assuming he'd die. She wanted a life with him. Granted, she wasn't familiar with every detail of him. But what she knew, she liked.

He was kind, observant, eager to please... except regarding seeding his wife, intelligent, and so handsome, it hurt to think of his looks for too long. He was rather quick to lash out with his friends, but it was not too dangerous.

He'd known Harry would duck, right? He'd purposefully thrown a butter knife and not his dagger at his hip. Volatile, but not murderous. He cared. If he didn't, none of those men would dine with him, and his servants wouldn't care about him. He provided satisfactorily. Managed his house well. He gave his staff advantages like education.

His knock startled her out of her thoughts. She sprang up, "Enter, please."

His entrance mirrored his arrival on their first night. But instead of striding toward her in sure steps, he leaned back, crossed his arms, and planted a boot against the closed door. His facial expression sent a spidery hand up her bare extremities.

"Won't you come to bed?" She asked, all her plans washing away under his gaze. Gone were the clothes he had on at dinner. He wore his night garments, or underthings. A light shirt, those dark pants, but with boots. What was it with him and those shoes? Didn't he ever take them off?

"I shall, but first we have things to discuss." His scrutiny flicked to each side of her, "Do you not have a shawl or covering?"

She held her head higher, her jaw tightening, "No."

"I'll buy you one. Every lady should have a robe lest she is awakened suddenly or catches a chill as she prepares for bed." He sighed, closing his eyes for a moment. When he opened them, it was only halfway. "First, never complain to my men again, unless I do something violent or so horrid I should be beaten to death."

She pressed her lips together, ignoring the pain from the wound still smarting there. Was this what he was like when he was angry? So calm? Regarding her coldly as he told her what to do?

"Second, I shall reiterate my reasoning. Your next husband deserves enough of my respect to keep you intact. He will receive my most prized and beautiful possession to care for in my stead. It is only right he gains you without worry you might be carrying our child. Or always comparing him to me."

His words hit her in the gut, one punch at a time. His most treasured item. Would she compare her new spouse to him? Yes.

"Thirdly, if you have... cravings... and are wont to sate them. Tell me how you used to and I shall purchase the means." With this, his stoic, haughty look faded into the embarrassment that filled his voice.

"How kind of you, husband." She didn't know what to think. "Just how am I to sate desires, exactly?" Virsin asked to give herself time to make sense of his demands.

He looked anywhere but at her. "Where we were stationed, the native women there had... tools for themselves. Or so I am told. They used them when their men departed for hunts or for war."

She would have to research these playthings. She was unaware those existed. "Oh. I've had nothing like those." Virsin paused, thinking over his points. "You called this a discussion, so may I speak?"

"Of course." Reg finally looked at her, the crease between his brows appearing again. "You never have to ask me for permission. For anything."

"But you just scolded me for going to your men with my concerns, did you not?"

"I-I did." He ran a hand over his hair as he said, "That is not what I intended. What I meant was I hope, in the future, you talk to me before them. Talk to other women, or your maid, about more personal matters."

"So you won't get beaten to death with their words and teasing, my lord husband?" Virsin tilted her head to the side and mimicked how he'd been when he entered by crossing her arms.

His lips twisted toward his scar, "Trust me, as soon as you invite your friends over, I shall return the favor."

She hated to tell him she only had one that would tease her. The others were mere acquaintances and were more likely to bite her in the back than be friendly.

"Do you not think my second husband would be kind, and understanding enough, to know that I would not be intact? If you choose him, wouldn't you want him to find me attractive? If he hears of you not touching me in any way, would it not make him wonder if he had the right to do so over you?"

Reg's brows notched upward with each question. "Well, I…" he started, then muttered under his breath as he turned, "I didn't think about that." He paced in front of her door. He snapped his fingers, "Ah, in the letter, I will explain he is much more deserving of you than I. That should deter him from not touching you."

Virsin countered with, "Or, my lord husband, if he knows I'm intact, wouldn't he immediately assume a problem exists with me and not even agree to keep me as you wish? But hate me, or find me disgusting because something is obviously so wrong with me you couldn't bring yourself to mount your own wife."

"I beg your pardon! Tis not what is going on here!" He stopped, turning on his heel to stalk her way. He towered over her, "There is nothing flawed in you. You are far from repulsive and if someone could hate you, then I shall kill them with my bare hands." He paused, eyes searching hers. Then he stepped back, and continued backward toward the doorway as he shook his head, "Well played, my lady. Well played indeed… Sin."

With the nickname she thought he would utter when they were both sated, he closed the door between them.

Chapter 16
One of These Plans Has to Come Together

Failure was the bitter taste in her mouth upon hearing the disturbing news. She had to pull out a map to devise where he and his regiment were being sent to. The discussion of training he and his favored men had the previous evening was actually a planning session for travel.

From now on, she would keep that code in her memory.

"I shall be back within a fortnight, if all goes well." Regus stated as they ate breakfast together.

She prodded at the fried egg. "During the grand conversation last night, you couldn't be bothered to tell me you would depart today? For fourteen days?!"

He chuckled, "I can hardly think when in your presence. I'm proud to speak what I did."

She still had hope. But it would be a fortnight before she could stoke it into something more worthwhile. After he ate, and the maid took away her pecked-at plate, Virsin followed him out to the courtyard. To complete her disappointment, the loading of the supply wagons was finished, and half his company were already mounted and in position.

Virsin bit back the childlike questions she wanted to ask him. The 'do you really have to depart?' and the 'but can't you just send your men and have Harry command them?' and the most childish 'can I go with you?' fell dead on her tongue.

"Do not fear, my lady wife. I have a list of gentlemen in my office, Mervas knows where it is, and he is to help you choose a suitable replacement for me if something should happen." Regus smiled as if he was giving her the best news.

"That is not what she wants to hear, I assure you." Slayth scowled, stopping his wide gray speckled steed beside them.

"Bestow a kiss upon your wife, and tell her you shall see her soon."

"Truth. Then give her a kiss from me, too." Harry winked, leaning forward on his horse's withers.

She watched as other men mounted their steeds without saddles upon them. Just blankets. "Isn't that uncomfortable?"

"Sometimes. We ride easier. And often get there right after our first delivery of supplies." Reg answered, ignoring his men's teasing.

"Half of us are dragonkin, and need better access to our horses to keep them from fearing us." Harry added, patting the thick black neck of his horse. "Something about our scent blending with theirs…" he trailed off and shrugged.

"You're dragonkin?"

"I am. So are Charn and Doxy, from the ones you've met. Slayth is well over four hundred years old, on his third wife, and third round of little Slayths. He's an elfkin." Harry added.

Slayth rolled his eyes to the gray skies, "Listen here dragon breath, I'll have you know she's my fourth wife, and I have only sixteen children."

"Only." Reg and Harry said together.

Slayth huffed, then turned his attention to Virsin, "We will make sure he comes back to you in one piece so you can finally give me a bouncing human baby with soft cheeks to hold."

"Slayth!" Reg barked, stopping his check over of his gear on his white horse. As if in agreement, the equine stomped its hoof and snorted.

"Give her a kiss," Harry barked right back at Reg. "Gods kick him."

Virsin stepped forward, tapping Reg on the arm. She wondered why they weren't wearing their armor yet. She met his gaze, peeking over his shoulder.

With a sigh, he turned and placed his lips on her forehead, "Stay well, my wife."

He jumped up into his saddle.

Virsin fisted her hands in her skirts to keep from pulling him back down off his horse. "Return to me."

Reg didn't answer her, but Slayth did as they trotted to the head of the column of soldiers, "He will, my lady!"

Each day, between household paperwork and chores, she penned another plan. Her husband would crawl into her arms and give her her first sexual experience. He was perfect for it.

All aspects of the main male characters she liked were in her stubborn spouse and made up his appearance. He only lacked mysteriousness, and the need to stay inside her every waking moment like they did.

"One day," she said, as she added the latest plan to the rest of the pile. Twenty. One of them had to work. Virsin had to convince him she was his wife and his alone, to live in the present and think for himself. Or at least do as she wanted.

Mervas entered the office, tea tray balanced on one hand and the letters in the other. "My lady, I thought you might enjoy some tea. It has been a while since breakfast. And you have not eaten lunch."

"I was just thinking some would be nice, Mervas, thank you." She smiled at the older gentleman and took the tray from him, shushing his sputters in protest. Setting it down atop the table between the two couches, she accepted the letters from him.

Opening the first one, she listened to the tea pouring into her cup, and Mervis rearranging the biscuits on their plate, before presenting her with both on the table, easily within her reach. "How many days has it been, Mervis?"

Each day she asked. And each day he answered.

"Eleven days, my lady."

"Hm. Has the Duke's chambers been refreshed?"

"Yes, we aired the room out. Tomorrow, we will wash the linens and dust."

"Thank you, Mervis." Her gaze flicked up to double check he had actually exited once the door clicked shut. She flopped back, tossing the letter on the cushion beside her unread.

Earlier that day, Bea had revealed Regus had few dalliances with women, and most Mervis knew about were professionals relieving the stress of war. At least she wouldn't be compared to some other lady. But a woman of boundless knowledge of the appetites of men was a formidable foe. That presented no added pressure. No, not at all.

"You best return early." She told his desk, squatting in the center of the room before the large bay windows with crimson curtains. "You said within a fortnight, not a fortnight, sir."

She closed her eyes, listing the first five plans and their steps within her mind. Each designed for a particular arrival. If he were to arrive in the morning, she would merely run to him and jump in his arms, then drag him toward the bedchamber. In the flurry, she would undress him before he could stop her, and one thing would lead to another.

If in the afternoon, Virsin would welcome him with a kiss on the cheek, hook her arm in his, and listen to his stories as they walked to his chambers. She'd let him rest, then sneak into his room and crawl into bed with him.

If Reg were to arrive home in the evening, she would make him come to her quarters. Bea and she had practiced how long it would require for her to get undressed for him. As long as he doesn't rush by taking the steps two at a time or running down the halls, she would have plenty of time.

She slept in his bed every night, just in case he arrived. A man saying no to a woman while both were naked? Hardly likely.

Yes, he slept in the nude. Bare. Free. Mervas finally revealed this information after considerable coaxing and incentives. He liked lemon squares. Those and the oat bread Fince loved had them turning a blind eye to her sleeping in their master's chambers after the first week had passed.

She picked up the letter and read it. Her father's report on the goings on of her old home. Nothing had changed. She put it to the side, sat up to grab another and open it. Settling back against the couch with her tea in her free hand, she skimmed over the invitation.

Virsin wasn't about to go to a ball or gathering of any sort, other than a tea party perhaps, without her husband.

She returned it to the table and took a sip before opening an additional letter. The hot liquid spluttered out between her lips and nearly jumped down the wrong pipe. Her husband's scrawl told her the date of his arrival, and nothing more.

Tomorrow.

Chapter 17
Is That a Sign of Happiness

His arrival, if in the morning, meant she was in her emerald dress. He'd liked it enough to work out his frustrations on the training grounds. It would be good enough to work them out on her this time.

She sat in the drawing room, the one with the window facing the long, winding drive through their forest. During his absence, she had noticed many things she loved about her home. The expanse of wilderness all around them. Obscuring the city view.

She could obtain anything quickly, her dukedom bordering the city.

What if he was hurt?

Surely, he would have told her in the letter. He had plenty of room to scratch out those details. She frowned, glaring at no tree in particular. How could she get him to write better letters?

Virsin poured hours into hers, never less than three pages. Four was too expensive to post. Three was perfectly adequate.

He wrote one page. No, half a page. Sometimes one line in response. Miserly. That's what he was, a fault to be corrected before his next trip.

She had to admit; he was only stingy in penned words.

In everything else, he gave above what he ought.

Something stirred dust on the lane. She stood, pressing her face against the cool glass. Excitement trilled through her bones and she could hardly keep still enough to gain the first peek of her... deer.

It was a pretty little thing. All thin legs and swinging ears to hear anything around her. But it was not her husband.

He and his men wouldn't be a puff on the lane, she admonished herself as she slouched in the chair, back at the tea table. With their number, they would be a dust storm, as they were the last time they rode out.

She glanced at the clock above the fireplace, then returned her attention to the window. It was nearly noon.

Virsin sighed. She'd really hoped he would arrive in the morning. She liked this plan the best, for it had her hands on him. All over him.

Heat filled her cheeks at the thoughts crossing her mind.

Noon struck, and Virsin rose as a maid entered to take her watch. The lane was to be within someone's eye at all times. Nothing would surprise her.

Climbing the stairs to her chambers, Bea then helped her into her afternoon garments. It was a thin thing she had recently bought. Tailored perfectly to her form, it wasn't as jaw dropping as the taunting emerald, but it was close. And it was easy to slip off. Not near as heavy as most of her other dresses.

One day, she hoped to test her husband's strength with this dress. See if he might rip it off her in the heat of his passion for her. Virsin fanned herself, hating how she got all blotchy when excited for him.

The afternoon passed with her playing with her lunch for an hour and a half, before finally conceding and allowing the torn apart meat pie to be taken away. She wondered if it would be salvageable for the poor, of if she had wasted food. Dogs, it could feed Reg's dogs.

She loved them, too. One slender hound called Nex, and a fuzzy shepherd named Lex. Visiting the stable animals tempted her, but she risked missing his arrival.

Besides, her fifth plan was for him to introduce her to all the animals and teach her to ride horseback.

He didn't know she knew all the horses and dogs, and the single nanny goat already. She was pretty sure her ability to ride had never come up either. Virsin was sure enough in her riding capabilities she could safely pull off her scheme with little bodily harm to herself.

Afternoon crawled into evening, and she faced her dreadful plan. It was the worst. Virsin was unable to wait around naked in her chambers. Suppose a servant had a query. Or took it upon themselves to serve her tea and biscuits?

She had the robe he'd bought for her and had arrived the day after he left. Silly man, stopping his regiment to purchase a present for his wife, back home. She shook her head; she couldn't wait around wearing just that either. Dreadfully unfashionable.

Virsin, as night fell, doubted his calculations' accuracy or if something had gone awry. She stood in the entryway, looking out the wide-open doors into the courtyard. The darkness was cool, the scent lingering like rain, and the beasts were filling the air with their sounds.

"Wonder if I should sing like the bugs and frogs, maybe then he'd follow my voice and hurry home." She rolled her eyes at herself and closed the doors. She smiled at Mervas, "Don't stay up all night waiting for him, I'm sure he wouldn't want you to exhaust yourself."

"Yes, my lady. You get some rest, too."

"I shall." She tapped her bottom lip, finally healed, as she climbed the stairs, at least until woken by something hard, warm, and curling around her deliciously.

In her dream, the ship she was in jostled and grew suddenly warmer on her left side. A sultry breeze made a strand of hair tickle her ear. The wind called her name?

She blinked, staring at the inky darkness of the bedchamber, and gasped as light bloomed to her left.

"Virsin?"

Ah, the musical tones she missed hearing these past weeks. "Reg?" She yawned, sitting up and stretching her arms over her head. The linens fell to her lap in perfect timing with the arch of her back.

"What are you doing?" His voice rose a few pitches, and the candle shook in his fingers.

She reclined, observing him. All of him, for having naught a stitch on. "Waiting for you, my lord husband." Her mouth ran dry, but her lower self certainly did not.

"Am I in your chambers?" He raked a hand through his hair, staring wildly about.

"No, come to bed, love." She patted the emptiness beside her.

Oh, she had a feast for her eyes. Pity there was only one light. He had nice equipment, not that she knew if it was the correct size. She supposed straight, like his, was best, wasn't it? The novels varied widely on what the males should sport for pleasure, but she was pretty sure "straight" was the consensus.

"You're naked." His gaze whipped back to her.

"As are you," she added, pulling the linens down, inviting him again to lie beside her.

He fumbled with the candle before slamming it down on his nightstand. He picked something up; swiftly, one leg went into his trousers.

Oh no, he didn't.

She lunged, covers hindering progress, then crawled to his side. She grabbed a handful of his pants, glaring up at him, "Don't."

"Virsin..." His deep voice held a warning tone, "I am too tired to have control. Please, another time."

Promising. Someday. Was it satisfactory for now? No. "Reg, I've waited long enough. My control is in the wind. Please."

His chest heaved in a heavy sigh, his grip on his pants loosened, and they let the soft fabric drop back to the floor.

Her study trailed down and noted he had gotten longer and somewhat thicker. Or did it seem that way since it was slightly at attention? Kind of like a man leaning over a table while seated at it.

"Move to the middle, love."

She did as she was told, scooting back while still watching him. Her heart skipped as he placed his hands on the bed, his hair falling forward in a wave of soft brown. She gasped when he lunged. The chamber turned inky black again. And stifling.

Tight bands were around her, making her curl in on herself, so her chin rested on her knees and her arms were pinned at her sides.

He was muttering incoherently above her. She strained to hear him, as she tried wriggling free. The covering for the bed. He'd caught her with the bedspread. How had she not seen that coming?

She giggled as she realized something. He couldn't carry her all the way to her room. He had to keep her here. And she was bound to liberate herself.

The bands left. Her stomach leapt to her throat, and she landed on her ass. The thick bedspread softened her fall, yet a bruise remained inevitable.

"Go to your rooms." Reg growled far above her, then his door slammed.

She swatted herself free of the covers. Clutching it and glancing around for any wandering servant. She was alone in the hall. She stood, stumbling on the cover until she managed to gather it in a way that allowed her to walk modestly.

She tried the handle. It didn't budge. "Welcome home, husband." She whispered to the door.

"Go to bed, Virsin." He said slowly from the other side.

"Drat," she hissed and padded barefoot along the cool stones of the hall to her room.

Chapter 18
Not to Sleep, but to Think and Curse

He listened intently. The soft pad of her feet down the hall, followed by the swish of the bedspread on the carpet in the middle, let him know he was safe. What had she been thinking? Naked, in a man's bed, it made no sense! Along with his palms, he rested his head against the dark wood of his thick door. He had to calm down.

Otherwise, he would unlock his door, go to hers, rip it open and try to make it all make sense. The worst thing he could possibly do. She didn't need him pawing at her. Embarrassing her. No, that wasn't what he was going to do.

The weight of his body felt triple what it was as he turned away from the path that would lead him to his wife. Each step to his bed was restricted under his need to be with her, understand her, and see if that flush could go all the way down or it was only for her cheeks and ears.

No. That wasn't right either. He shook his head as he finally reached the side of his bed again. He fell into it, hugging the pillow under his face.

It smelled like her. Regus turned his hips, bringing a knee up to relieve the pressure on his hard cock. He pushed the pillow away and filled his nose with her scent on his sheets. Gods, she was everywhere.

Regus rolled to his back, splaying wide in the middle to stare up at the dark timbers of his ceiling.

She had said, 'welcome home, husband' and that nearly had him jerking her back inside. What was it with those three words? Or was it that she was naked, in his bedding, on the other side of the door he barely locked before she tried the handle? Ladies of the capital were wily.

What would have happened had he lay down? Fallen asleep? Would he wake with her... he growled, sitting up in bed and pinching the bridge of his nose. Was this what insanity felt like? Was this the reason his cousin bragged about his wife's rides every opportunity he had?

The queen.

He stared at his door, as if looking right at Virsin. They were cousins. That was where his precious wife had been brainwashed. Queen Lythaine had taught his wife that she needed to ride that often, that well, and make children. If he could convince her to become herself again, then she wouldn't come to his bed again. Right?

He had to talk to Fedvich.

Regus lay back down, staring up at the ceiling before squeezing his eyes closed, as a part of him definitely wasn't at rest and wouldn't be for a while. It was useless to take care of it now. He'd have to again when he woke, for he knew his wife would be in his dreams.

"What do you mean undo a brainwashing?" Fedvich paused, his brows drawn low over his eyes, one hand holding the worn honing tool while the other kept his sword balanced on his knee.

Regus glanced at the others, most were doing their own thing, far enough away they shouldn't overhear their conversation. "She thinks she has to ride me. That's brainwashing."

The redhead stared, then slowly placed his sword and honing tool down on the table before folding his hands on top of them. "Is that so? Go on, explain this... phenomenon to me."

If anyone should know what was taught to ladies, it would be Fedvich. "You've done it."

"Have I?"

Regus gritted his teeth, working his jaw muscles to keep the harsh words at bay. His patience grew thinner and thinner these days. "How do you undo your teachings on what a lady should provide her husband?" His vision crossed on Fedvich's sword point, that was a little too close to the tip of his nose. He followed the blade up, meeting the sex expert's eyes over the metal.

Fedvich tilted his head, chin jutted, regarding his lord and commander with narrowed eyes, "Regus, I heighten the natural abilities and desires of ladies so they can share such things with their husbands. And for the last blessed time! I did not train your wife!"

He flicked the blade away, glaring just as much as Fedvich did at him, "Then whoever trained her, be it the queen or her own mother, taught her that she must perform such duties even if it makes her sick."

"Has she made a face at you? Dry heaved?" Tempered threats threaded Fedvich's voice.

"No, but-"

"Is there fear rolling off her in waves when you enter the room?"

"No. Tha-"

"Then, for the love of gods man, get it through your thick skull that the lady wants you. Truly."

He stared down the redhead, debating on if he should attack and pin the man down until he let the secrets spill about his training practices. "But sh-"

"No."

"Fedv-"

"Fuck her."

"She doesn't wa-"

"Yes, she does." Fedvich said, looking down the length of his blade at Regus' chin. "And before you begin to make excuses in that brain of yours, answer me these things..." Fedvich smirked, putting his sword back in its sheath before pulling out its twin. He studied the blade for a moment before working it over the whetstone. "Didn't she bring you lunch of her own accord?"

"Yes."

"Didn't she wear a rather revealing and embarrassing dress that day in hopes you'd partake?"

"That wasn't-"

"I promise that was her intention. And should she wear that barely there thing again, it will be the same intention of getting you between her legs." Fedvich studied him for a moment, "And I suppose she did something similar last night?" The twist to the redhead's lips added mischief to his countenance, "Did our poor Duke Vicious have to take care of the mini duke by himself because he denied his own wife?"

"I don't know why I talk to you."

"I don't either, because I never give you the advice you want to hear."

Regus snorted, then shook his head. Watching Fedvich work, he questioned, "Are you sure she is acting based on her own desires and not on some predetermined notion of what she should be doing?"

"Do ladies have the same basic instinct and desires as men? Yes. Yes, she wants you. Forget all those times Slayth and Bertran said you weren't what women looked for. You should know by now they said those things so they wouldn't have a thousand miniature yous running around, not that you are in any way lacking." Fedvich glared at him, "For you are certainly not lacking by any means." He smirked then, "Take it from me, who knows every inch. She'll enjoy it more than I did."

Chapter 19
Small Steps for Big Rewards

The next two days, her husband avoided her like she was a disease and he susceptible. On day three, a new plan emerged. For she knew now which servants invariably tipped him off to her whereabouts.

Mervas, the traitor, and a little errand boy who was always somewhere near his master.

She tapped a finger on her lip, watching the child dance in place at the end of the stairs, which blocked her from going to his office. Virsin realized Reg had probably hired the boy for this specific purpose, not to perform errands. Clever. Annoying, but clever.

Fince, her ever loyal partner, had kept the boy supplied with tea, sweets, and water.

He bolted, running for the first-floor bath.

Virsin gathered her skirts and ran up the stairs. The new thin dress was a wonder. She could run so much faster in it than the others. She desperately wanted to try pants. Perhaps she could even outrun Reg's long legs if she had a decent pair of trousers.

She hit his office threshold, fumbled the knob, then shot inside. She closed the door behind her and leaned back. Virsin gave herself a moment to catch her breath.

"How did yo-" He cleared his throat, "Wife."

Oh, so he was going to act like he hadn't seen her in nearly three days, nor the fact they'd been naked together the last time? She could play the game, too. "Reg, I've missed you."

He flinched, literally and visibly. Then red tinged his neck and ears under his messy pile of hair. "I-I- that's nice."

"Nice? Is it?" Maybe she wouldn't play the game as a new idea came to her. She trailed her fingers over the curved carved top of the couch as she made her way to him. "One would think inducing a sense of loneliness in another person was a sin."

Virsin jumped her fingers to the corner of his desk. Trailed them along the smooth edge of the dark, polished wood. "I'm beginning to believe it is the worst feeling in the world. The longing for my husband. Solitude. Especially since he threw me out of his room."

She lent to her voice a sultry tone. Or what she hoped was a sensual tone. She wasn't sure what that particular tone should sound like.

Rounding the corner, she watched him lean back in his seat, as if trying to push away from his desk, and, in turn, her. Unfortunately, for him, she added an extra rug just last night, hindering the scooting ability of that particular chair. She perched on the edge, crossing her legs toward him. The tip of her shoe she trailed up and down his thigh in slow strokes. "What are you going to do about your painful actions, husband?"

His Adam's apple bobbed, and he closed his eyes. His hands clutched the chair arms as if they were his life raft. "You should not have been in my room. I had every right to throw you out."

He sounded strangled.

"And making me miss you, what about my pain caused by you?" She leaned further toward him. The satisfaction of seeing him nervous and licking his lips when he opened his eyes to her so close to him made her smile.

"Virsin, forgive me. I've been so busy catching up on business I haven't been able to eat meals with you. That will be remedied soon."

"You must be so tired. You look flushed." She slid off the desk, pressing her palm against his forehead. "You're not too hot." She murmured, then hugged him to her chest. "Not hot enough at all. Not for a fever, at least."

He jerked, trying to pull away.

Virsin smiled, dramatically using his struggle to fall into his lap. "Shall I help you work?" She kicked her feet as they dangled over his arm, making sure the movement settled her deeper in her delicious seat.

His breath hissed in between his teeth, "Must I remind you we are to be..."

"To be?" She blinked slowly up at him, and asked softly, "Riding?"

In a single swift move she was in the air, he was standing, and they were moving. Virsin clutched his muscular upper arm, one hand fisting in his lapel. His hold disappeared, and her ass hit the couch. He may have relinquished her, but she hadn't loosed him.

The momentum of him dropping her pulled him down with her.

He saved himself at the last minute by using the sofa's back. She dangled from his shoulder and lapel, legs spread wide to accommodate his body as his knee pressed into her skirts. She tugged and arched, nearly there.

Her lips brushed his chin, and his the tip of her nose. Then he twisted away. His jacket limp in her clutches.

She replayed his move mentally. How was that even possible? His back was to her, his hands flat on his desk, and his head hung.

Another opportunity popped into her mind, and she leapt up from the couch. But slowed as she gained her feet. She needed to approach him carefully. She held his coat in both hands.

Virsin placed the garment over his shoulders, pressing herself against his back as much as she could as she slid her palms down his biceps. Glorious body. Firm. He smelled good, too.

"You never told me what we are to be, my love."

"Riding." He shook his head, "No, not that. Working. We need to work."

He straightened, effectively shrugging her off. "I have business to attend to. Don't wait for me."

"Wha-" She watched him leave, and whimpered. "So close." She pressed her fingers to a growing ache in the middle of her forehead. "Will this incur another two days of loneliness?"

Chapter 20
Stick It in Me

Regus was good at keeping his word for most of his vows, still. They began having meals together again the next day. Virsin waited. Patiently. It was two days before she started another action plan.

Her cleavage display proved ineffective.

The stubborn mule of a spouse must be a hip and thigh man.

One of the old fashions had slender skirts. A few years after the slimming, the fashionistas had introduced slits. Scandalous. She still had three of those dresses. While she wasn't fond of her own thighs, they were too jiggly she feared, but if he liked them... then by all means he should partake in any way she could get him to.

Virsin sauntered into breakfast and instead of sitting in her seat, she sat on the table at his side. The slit opened, revealing both, and one all the way up to her hip when she crossed her legs away from him. She swung her foot gently as she plucked a cherry from his plate and popped it into her mouth.

She waited for Mervas to shoo the servants out of the room before asking, "Did you sleep well, my love?"

Regus' lips were twisted, as if he'd stopped in mid chew but also wanted to say 'oh.' He took his napkin, wiping his mouth as he leaned back into the corner of his chair, farthest away from her. His eyes widened when he realized his mistake. Now he had the best view of his wife's legs.

"I did. Did you?" His voice was hoarse.

"Not really. I was cold." She pretended to shiver. "You're always so blissfully hot. I bet I could sleep well next to you. Warm. Cozy."

"I sleep hot." He winced and slowly turned his head away.

"We are a perfect match, wouldn't you say? Shouldn't we see how beautiful we are in bed together? Sleeping?"

"Virsin, no. You know you are to save yourself for my replacement."

"That is your decision. Not mine."

His gaze shot back to hers, "What do you mean? You want to be alone after I die? I cannot promise you I can find a man willing to take you if I-I've... I've stuck it in you." His face flushed with his speech, and he covered his face with his palms. "Woman, you are quickly becoming a thorn in my side."

"If only you would be a thorn in my core." She grinned as he peeked at her from between his fingers.

"Are you a virgin? Some things you say... and do..." Regus floundered, and slid his hands down to rest them on his knees.

"If I claimed no, can we end this farce?"

"Yes." He said, then shook his head, "No! That isn't the... it..." He cursed under his breath, twice. "I have somewhere to be."

"Curse your long legs." Virsin said with venom, watching him basically run out of the room. "Where?!" she called after him.

"Taking a lengthy walk in a large lake." She heard him yell back.

She had a pause, picturing him rising out of the water all wet and... she slid off the table and ran after him. "Truly?" Virsin asked, catching him at the entrance to their home.

"You followed me?" He shook his head, "No. I... I have training."

"Oh good, I want to watch." She strode down the lane, not giving him a chance to lock her in the house. Not that he ever did, but she didn't doubt he would.

"Have fun."

She whirled, "What? Where are you going now?"

"I remembered I have an appointment in the city." He whistled sharply, a signal he wanted his horse, then he ran toward the stables.

After watching him ride his stallion like he was trying to escape hell, Virsin decided she needed a walk, and some kind of exercise. Despite the overcast sky, she didn't detect the scent of rain and assumed it would stay away for some time. At least, she hoped. She heard Harry's voice loud and clear as she approached the training grounds and noted the doors were wide open again. Upon entering, gazes swung toward her from the soldiers sitting, listening to the lesson Harry was giving.

Her appearance didn't disrupt too much. They were getting used to her being around, it seemed.

Doxy rose, trotting over to her with a smile. He waited until he was at her side before asking, "Are you looking for our lord?"

"No, he ran away from me to town." Virsin said, crossing her arms over her chest to keep from letting loose the rant forming in her mind.

"Oh." Doxy shifted from one foot to another as he looked from Harry back to her, and then back again. "Is there anything I can do?"

"Go back to your lesson. I'll listen in, too." She smiled, reaching over to pat his rounded cheek. She veered to one side, taking a seat on one of the benches they had moved to the edge of the training grounds to make room for their exercises after Harry's instruction.

Only, it wasn't quite the lesson she was expecting.

The men got up, formed lines, and made sure they were all equally spaced. Tights. They were wearing tights. All of them.

Luckily they were all wearing their shirts, too, or Virsin would have seen more of the boys than she needed.

Voices melded together in a spritely tune as they moved as one in a series of steps, spins and gestures.

Harry grinned as he made his way over to her, "You are looking delicately delicious today, my lady. Have you finally rode our lord so well he's comatose in bed?" He asked as he sat down beside her. He took a pair of gloves from his boot top, and tugged them on before twisting his metal bit laden hair onto the crown of his head.

"No such luck, but thank you for noticing my efforts." Virsin watched the men dance. For a dance it was. "What is going on?"

Slayth vanished, returning with three apples—one for Harry, one for her, and one for himself—then perched on a nearby table. "Still no luck, I gather?" He asked around a bite of the apple.

"Nope." Harry answered for her, studying the green flesh of his fruit before taking a bite himself. "Practice, for when we begin our second jobs."

Slayth snorted at their backs "Damn that boy. I still don't understand his illogical stubbornness in this."

"Oh yes, as he is usually so logical and not emotional at all." Harry stated drolly with a roll of his eyes. He turned toward her on the bench and said, "Reg didn't have a rough childhood, not until his father passed. He was fifteen or so, maybe seventeen. I think that is why this is... such an issue. His mother took it terribly hard."

"Enough to take her own life a mere two years later." Slayth added quietly.

Virsin's heart broke for the boy Regus had been.

Harry shot him a glare. "Not our story to tell."

"You started it." Slayth lifted a shoulder, taking another bite of his apple.

"Just to try to soothe her!" Harry motioned to Virsin, still glaring at Slayth. "Not make her sob. Tactics, sir."

Slayth raised his brows. "Tact, not tactics."

"You've been hanging around Charn too much, old man. I need no corrections." Harry turned back to Virsin, "Don't take this the wrong way, but are you... hard up?"

"Tactics nor tact there." Slayth reprimanded.

"How do you mean?" Virsin asked, jumping when Harry made a vulgar motion with his hand in Slayth's face and the elder snapped his teeth near a digit.

"I mean, are you burning or so wound up your body hurts?" Harry studied his middle finger before returning his attention to Virsin.

Virsin nodded, experiencing the embarrassment of admitting such things. But he had asked...

"Tell her about the trick," Slayth suggested as he nudged Harry with the toe of his boot planted on Harry's shoulder as he lay back across the table.

"I am!" Harry pushed the heavy shoe off him and brushed the shoulder of his tan tunic off, and muttered under his breath about how he couldn't find good help these days. "You ought to do something far more provocative. It's certain to make him lose control and finally break his pointless vow. We think you should do your usual masturbation in his rooms when he's bound to find you."

Her cheeks heated more than they ever had as she claimed, "I have never and I cannot!" She glanced back at the dance, better that than the men around her. "Provocative like dancing? And what second job?"

Slayth said disdainfully, "I dislike this era. Women are too suppressed."

"Well, I think now is the time to begin." Harry talked over Slayth's complaint, then added, "We're going to start a troupe so we can still pay the bills and not be... well, getting fat and lazy." He paused, staring at her face. "Wait... do you know how to masturbate?"

Virsin groaned as soon as he said the word 'wait' and covered her face in her hands. "I've read about things in novels."

"Explains some of her drive," Slayth stated around a mouthful of apple. "Though, I have yet to see a passage in these romance novels give details worth teaching."

Harry's shoulders dropped in a sigh. He looked at his hands, then smiled to himself as he broke his apple in half. He'd only taken the one bite, while Slayth was nearly done with his. "Look here, I'll teach you," He tossed the bitten part behind him, hitting Slayth on his forehead. He grunted when Slayth cursed him, but scooted close to Virsin, avoiding another boot to his side effectively. "Pretend this is your area between your legs." He cupped the half in his palm.

"That's not a good visual."

"Shut your mouth, Slayth. You want to play show and tell instead?" Harry shot a look over his shoulder.

"Nope. Continue." Slayth waved a dismissive hand, eating Harry's discarded half.

Harry ran a finger down the center line, "Here is your slit, opening. Where the seeds are is your hole, the one Regus should've already entered, but... this will make him take it." Where the stem was, he stopped and began rubbing in small circles. "Up here, in a hood, you'll find a little knot, or bump. Once you hit it, you'll feel real good, so rub it like this. Start slow, build up. Your body will guide you; trust your instincts."

Virsin wondered why her mouth was watering, and her belly warmed suddenly.

He tapped the center of the apple, where the seeds were. "There are more spots inside, not bumps, but areas that are just as good to touch as the bump up here." As he spoke, he rubbed one seed up and down.

"Hmph, maybe apples aren't so bad of a visual reference after all." Slayth admitted, looking over Virsin's shoulder.

She jumped, not realizing he'd gotten so close. "And all this, three spots are in all women? I won't be searching for something that isn't there?"

Harry's face shifted into pity. "Oh, my lady, these are definitely on you and in you. Have you not explored yourself?"

"I..." Virsin began, but Slayth interceded.

"They're told it's sinful, remember?"

"Right. Piss and poop, that's all you're to do before a husband pops his seed in and you give birth." Harry then looked back at Virsin, "Try it. Do it by yourself first and get used to it, then go to his bedchambers and show him what you've learned." He grinned with the last bit, "Fool proof."

Chapter 21
No Madness in Her, But in Him…

Virsin ate dinner in her chambers. The rowdy men's riding tips left her completely drained. Her head was full of fresh ideas. She had to pique his interest; otherwise, all the advice they had given her for her first time would be for naught.

Piecing together their suggestions, and the details from her romance novels, Virsin now had better understanding of what exactly went on between the bodies of a man and a woman.

She was desperate to experience it, to know him in such a way.

But before anything else, she needed to let all the information soak in.

In this castle, the bath was in a singular room, fitted for luxury. Servants had two rooms, one for men and the other for women. Guests had another set of chambers. And then, there were the washrooms shared by the lord and lady.

Virsin doubted she would ever bathe with her husband, seeing as how he was so averse to being naked or bothered by her.

In addition, Harry had been ever so kind as to describe a way she might relieve some of her frustration before Reg gave in to her. A long, hot bath, he'd claimed, provided the perfect cover for the task. He'd also assured her he knew many women who performed the act and did not go mad.

She trusted Harry as much as she was curious.

After she told Bea to return in two hours, she settled into the warm concoction. Relishing in the water mixed with goat's milk, and the petals of some flower which smelled sweet, Virsin allowed herself a moment of stillness. Her peace was shattered by a flood of thoughts.

What if he truly did not like her? Suppose he was in love with another woman. What if he was as stubborn as she and they would be in this stalemate for the rest of her life?

Virsin pushed the questions out with a long breath. Each time one reared its head, she thought of Reg's eyes. Or his smile. The night when the candlelight flickered over him, making her dreams more realistic.

The ache grew.

As if someone would sneak in without her notice, Virsin looked around the room. She sat up, slightly more, leaned back, and spread her legs with her knees somewhat elevated as Harry had instructed. Virsin slid her fingers between her lips in the water and began her search. It didn't take her long.

One touch and she gasped with a slight jerk. "Oh, that won't do."

She bit down, gently, on a knuckle. Drawing circles around the nubbin with the index finger, slow at first, then building momentum. Something sensual grew within her. She felt warm and tight all over. Her hips began moving in time, and she flung her hand out of her mouth to grip the side of the tub.

Water splashed, and she tilted her head back toward the tub's rim to avoid it choking her. She should smooth her breathing, it was quite ragged, like she had been running. But it was such a pleasant experience. What was echoing in the room? Must be her bath splashing to the floor.

She would clean it up before Bea returned.

A cry escaped her lips, her body thrust taut and nearly rising from the water. She was both tight and trembling at the same time. She didn't need to breathe, but needed breath to find more of whatever sensation this was.

"Virsin!" His voice thundered before the door flew open and clapped against the wall.

His sword flickered orange in the candlelight, held before him as if he was about to thrust it into an enemy.

Virsin grappled for something to cover herself with, water slipping through her fingers while gathering useless petals, "Reg!" She didn't sound at all like herself. Like some woman who'd ran the lane but was calling her lover's name at the same time.

His head tilted, sharp gaze flowing back and forth over the room. He stalked around, looking behind the door. As if anything or anyone could be behind it with the knob planted solidly in the wall.

He'd thrown it open too hard; the handle was stuck in the wall? What had she done so wrong? She followed him, sinking low into the creamy water, and hoping it wasn't as see through as she thought it was.

Wait.

Why did she care?

Reg was back at the threshold, having completed a full circuit of the bathing room. He held his sword loosely in one hand, his eyes glancing down at the floor as he picked up his boot and kicked the edge of a pool of her bathwater. "Was someone in here?"

"No." She licked her lips, not exactly sure how she should act in this situation. Did she have an advantage, or was she at his mercy?

Oh, if only she would stop panting, and feeling these odd little shocks down there and the warmth sputtering.

"Are you well? There were... sounds..." His gaze narrowed on her.

She could nearly read the calculations going through his mind about this strange situation. Virsin leaned back, settling in as if she was still relaxing. She rested her arms on the sides.

Immediately, his sight fell elsewhere.

"I am in good health. I wonder why you interrupted my... bath time." She couldn't very well say the act accomplished seconds before he crashed in. *Think, Virsin, think! How long had she been in there?*

"As I said, there were sounds that reminded me very much of an attack." Reg's mouth worked before he said, "I thought you were being attacked."

"I am not."

"Then what was going on?! There's been some kind of struggle." Reg snapped, his gaze hard on her again.

She didn't like his countenance. Not at all. The vexation of that look made her stand in the bath and place her hands on her hips, the bath water sheeted down her frame. "I am... finding... pleasure!" The indignation and irritation faded quickly with each of the words. Snuffing out her anger quicker than a bucket of water over a fire.

He shook his head, the crease between his brow returned in an instant, "Pleasure? How..." Then his eyes popped, before dropping to her waist. "I-" He cleared his throat, and his weapon trembled in his hold.

Regus turned on his heel, grabbing the doorknob but failing to grasp it. Failing further to once he held firm to pull the door from the wall. His sword clattered to the stones, and Reg situated his hand and shoulder between the thick wood and the wall, grunting with the effort. At long last dislodging it with a rather red face and shaking hands, he fumbled his sword up, finally just tossing it out into the hallway so he could slam the door shut behind him.

She sank back into the bath, curling in on herself. The opportunities missed in that opportune time played through her mind. "Drat it all." She muttered against her knees.

Chapter 22
Paperwork to Cool Off, a Drink to Warm Up

Adrenaline was a fickle beast. One moment it helped take down an enemy and the next it made it difficult to walk. His wife was the same. She bolstered him, gave him something to fight and think for other than his men. Then she turned around and crippled him. He was damned.

He had to think logically.

Virsin was a battlefield. One to protect. To leave unsullied. Not a battle field. A village. Yes, that worked better. A village that he took the battle away from. He should resolve to live elsewhere. Let her have the house.

See, that was logical. He surveyed the pile of paperwork on his desk. No, that wasn't logic, that was him being a coward. What man would leave all the work to his servants and wife?

Regus strode to the side table. He eyed the crystal bottles and jars. He hadn't a clue what were in each one of them. The red looked like wine, not enough. The brown, then. He plucked the top off it and drank three swallows from the fluted neck and hissed after swallowing them. He replaced the top and the bottle back on the silver tray.

His body reminded him of the aversion he had to alcohol with a full body shudder.

He returned to his desk, pulling a small drawer out from the middle, he fumbled for a peppermint and popped it into his mouth. While he sucked on it, he picked up his ledger and flipped it open to the last page he'd been working on balancing. The next bill mocked him from one of the smallest piles of papers before him. He eyed the larger towers of letters and reports.

Was there a way he could go back to being a baron?

His head throbbed, both of them. He groaned, resting his elbows on his desk as he pinched the bridge of his nose. There were things called stewards, people who ran households and all the business therein. He could hire one of those.

It also meant what the steward earned would be less money for Virsin's future.

That sound. It erupted in his ears once more. A soft cry. He knew now what it was. She made noises like that in pleasure.

This wasn't the train of thought he should be on.

"Enter!" He barked seconds after the knock sounded.

"Well, well, well, why are you still in your office?"

He glared at the redhead, "Obviously waiting on whatever it is you have to say."

"Touche." Harry chuckled, closing the door behind him. Something settled on his face, hooding his eyes, and he stayed near the threshold. "Are we well?"

Regus leaned back in his chair, "Are we?" What was it that Harry observed? What had he done behind his back? Harry lingered near exits only when feeling guilty or planning mischief.

"You still seem tense."

When Harry didn't expound, Regus returned, "Am I?"

"Fuck her, please. That is all I will ever ask of you! Fuck. Your. Wife." Harry threw his hands up in the air.

Regus watched his second, his brow twitching, "You came into my home to find out if I was deep in my wife? What was your plan if I was?"

"Celebrate with the boys because at last! At last, the Grand Lord Duke Regus of the Vicious partook of that pretty gorgeous creature he's married to. Married. Wedded. To wet a dick at any given moment because it's legal!"

"You lost the bet, didn't you?"

Harry deflated, "I did."

"Slayth?"

Harry heaved a sigh.

"After all these years, have you not learned that he knows me best and you shouldn't take up a bet he has on me?"

"Yeah, but he doesn't know your wife."

"And you do?"

Harry's face twisted back and forth between thoughtful and mischief. "That depends."

"On what?"

"If I say I know her, will you know her too? Or if I say that I don't, because I don't in the way you are thinking at this very moment, will you partake anyway because I haven't yet?"

Regus felt his jaw work, "Do you know how late it is for your games that make no sense?"

"Rather late, yes. Late enough that you should be making little grunting noises over your wife."

"Out."

"Do it! I shall await your report! Not too early in the morning. Let me know how many times she says your name!"

Regus cursed under his breath several times after the door slammed closed behind Harry.

Chapter 23
Don't Let the Water Grow Cold

Failure was not an option. She could use her lack of wit to her advantage, yet. Her father always mentioned striking while the iron was hot. Well, she hadn't let her body wrinkle in the bath.

It was good enough.

She pulled the robe he bought her on. Her chemise seemed so thin under it, compared to the rich embroidery on the blue fabric. It fit her perfectly. Down to the belt being wide, which she adored. She left her hair loose, as dry as it was going to be after being toweled.

She wanted to know what she would smell like after he had his hands on her.

Virsin exited her rooms and padded on bare feet to the second floor. It was then she realized the office was beneath their chambers. She waited outside his office, listening to him move around inside for a moment before opening the door a crack. "My lord husband?"

He turned as soon as she spoke, his hair framing his face, dark circles under his lashes and a tiredness clouded his countenance. "Virsin?"

"You should be in bed, it is late." She watched his eyes drop from hers, trail along her body, then back to the book in his hands. His swallow was as visible as it was audible.

"As should you. The robe looks good on you." He shut the tome after scanning it for a moment. He cursed under his breath, "I know not why I try when my mind is..." His eyes flew to her for the briefest of moments before swinging back to his desk.

Success was a sweet nightingale calling outside.

"Walk me to bed?" She leaned against the door, opening it wider as if inviting him to step out into the hall. She curled her toes in the carpet's warmth inside the office, away from the cold stone of the path she must retake. "Or shall I accompany you to yours?"

"You are going to catch your death walking around barefoot in the middle of the night." Regus shook his head at her and extinguished the candles on his desk before he did the same for those by the door. "Let's get you to bed."

He took her hand, closing the door behind them, and led her to the stairs.

She clasped his hand in both of hers, holding it close to her center. Each step caused him to brush against her or bump into her. Virsin asked, "Has something happened to cause you much work today?"

"I couldn't concentrate because..." Regus trailed off, the muscles in his hand and arm flexing. His free hand raked his hair back from his face and rested on top of his head as if the pressure could keep his thoughts from escaping.

She smiled, skimming her palm up his bare forearm to his rolled-up sleeves, "You didn't find me nor catch my orgasm until you were supposed to be done with your work, my love. My pleasure could not have been a distraction for you. I know you think naught of my needs."

Her heels dragged, and the smooth stone wall became her back rest. Waist constricted where his arm had clamped upon her. Her feet dangled. He brought their joined hands up above her head, and rested his forehead below them to look down on her.

Oh, my. Virsin tingled all over. *Yes, please, dear husband.*

His hair created a curtain, as if they were in their own world. She and him. With his body pressing hers against the wall, she wished she had heard of self-pleasure before.

She watched his jaw work. He was taking too long to do or say what he wanted. Perhaps he needed some aid. Virsin freed a leg from her robe with her uncaptured hand and pressed her thigh up over his hip. She debated on bringing the other up when his body shifted. A gasp flew from her lips as there was a delicious pressure against her still excitable womanhood.

"I am not as gentle as these thin hands of yours. Nor am I as soothing as the bath you were in. I assure you, what you think you want from me, you would rather have from the man you will spend most of your life with. As I've said before, many times. I will say this, if with me, you will find nothing but regret and heartache." With his last words, he pressed into her with a jerk of his hips and his hand squeezed her fingers painfully.

Virsin knew what he was saying. Her mind didn't care about words. The sensation of him against her, pressing and holding, had her ache return tenfold. She needed release. Rubbing. She hooked her leg further around him, gasping as another effect happened, the friction she desired of his tough pants against the edge of her robe and the tiny bit of chemise caught between them.

"Listen to me..." Regus began, interrupting himself with a curse under his breath. "You are a maddening woman. Every dream I have is you. Before you, I dreamed of one like you. A foul tongue, thick thighs, and not frail so I can fully enjoy..." His jaw cracked when he shut his mouth so hard his teeth clacked.

Cold assaulted her body. Her feet hit the floor, and she half slid, half caught herself on the wall. Virsin stared at him, too far away, nearly clear across the hall. "Regus..."

"Don't," he growled, slouching with his hand splayed over his crotch, but he looked at her with narrowed lids, his head cocked up.

If he had his sword, she felt she would be staring down its length. Duke Vicious was warning her his control was slipping. She tilted her chin up too, standing straight and tugging her belt loose. "You have seen me in less, husband, but does this chemise stir what is under your palm?"

His eyes followed the path of her robe to the floor. He stepped back as she stepped forward. Then again. His back brushed the wall, and he planted his feet shoulder width apart.

Her fingers clasped his wrist, tugging. She wanted to see. Virsin reached up.

Virsin's world spun as something hard knocked the air from her lungs when it hit her stomach. She grappled for a hold, pulling and gripping his shirt and hair until the heels of her hands found a small ledge in his belt. "Regus!" She hissed, watching the floor from higher than she'd ever been in a house, and backwards.

"You should be in bed."

His voice was harsh. Not quite like the general barking orders, but something just as dangerously dark. Electricity had her body trembling with his words. Surely, this was the moment.

A touch of nausea had her closing her eyes to keep from watching the hall in this way. It was a bit much. She registered the click of a door, his boots sounded different in softer carpet. "Oh gods," she caught herself saying as she felt her world spin again.

She hit something soft, bounced once, twice.

She cracked her eyes open in time to see her husband literally running out of her bedchambers.

Virsin screamed and beat her fists against the bed.

Chapter 24
Is That a Bell You're Wearing?

She knew she wouldn't see her husband the day after. Which was fine. Let him mull over her bath time on his own.

It should do him some good.

Virsin found herself less tense about her shoulders. At least she had a way to release tension. Especially if he was to keep himself from her.

The next day, she was surprised to find several of their furniture pads thicker. She could nearly bounce on them. The day after that, all cushions were plush. On the third, her husband was at the breakfast table.

Fascinating.

As they ate, she noted he seemed a bit... off. Odd. Something wasn't quite right. Was he finally struggling with his manhood in her presence?

Or in the three days since witnessing her first special bath, had he lain with someone who had given him a dreadful memento to remember them by on his privates? Did he have a wound from training?

Both options proved unsuitable, yet one transgression held less weight.

"My lord husband, is something the matter? Should I have Mervas call a doctor?" She asked, dabbing at the corners of her lips with her napkin.

"I am well, my lady."

His voice sounded strained. He was not fine. "Shall I guess, then? For you are not yourself." She leaned forward, placing her elbows on the table and hating herself for the rudeness of the action. Steepling her fingers, and tapping them against her chin, "Did you have relations with someone else?"

Reg snorted, "No."

His answer was too quick to be a lie. She tried not to be deterred by the relief making her breathe easier. Relief? This much, because he hadn't bedded another woman instead of her?

"Do you have an infection?"

His dark eyes stayed on her even as he shook his head slowly. "What is the sudden interest in my activities and wellbeing?"

"I have always been interested in your health. With your activities... you won't allow me to do much." Virsin batted her lashes as she pushed her bottom lip out.

No reaction.

"Then tell me, what is the matter? You squirm like a boy hiding candy he found, or the fact he damaged something precious." She paused a beat, "Could you imagine what our children could get into in this grand house?"

Reg's eyelids kept narrowing on her. With the last sentence, he scoffed, "The children here will be yours, but not mine, my lady."

Was there some emotion in play other than annoyance? Had she imagined that? "I am ready to receive your child any time you should choose, my lord husband." She watched him turn both pale and red at the same time. She believed such a feat only occurred in noble-born women like herself, following a cry. "Is it that your seed is not fruitful?"

"There is nothing wrong with my seed!" He rose from his chair, throwing his napkin down on his empty plate. "I'll be in my office should you require me."

"I always need you, my lord." Satisfaction curled her lips when he regarded her with a look over his shoulder. After he closed the door behind him, she slumped in her chair. "Thorn in his side indeed." She crossed her legs and swung her foot as she tapped a finger on her bottom lip. She wanted to give him time. Time to settle and think himself safe.

"I suppose I shall accept my lord's invitation." She stood and walked slowly from the dining hall, through the house, to the stairs. She trailed her fingertips over the polished wood of the banister, taking each step as if testing it. When she stood in front of his door, she took the time to smooth the narrow skirt and adjust the slit ever so slightly so it would do a better job of making her a rather large thorn.

Without knocking, she opened the door for herself and entered her husband's domain. She paused, noting he was standing at his desk with papers in hand instead of sitting. Virsin shut it behind her, both hands still on the knob as she tilted her hip and brought her knee up slightly by resting her foot on its toes. Entire leg bare for him.

"Wh-what are you doing here?"

With a shrug and tilt of her head, she said, "You said you would be here, and I am always in need of you."

"Virsin, stop this. I have work to do." Reg shook his head, returned his gaze to the sheaf of papers in one hand, and the single in the other.

"Yes, you do. Lots of work. Some of it carries into the night, your night work must carry into the day. You have much to catch up on. So far behind." Virsin tsked and pushed off the door to stalk toward her husband. She'd seen one of the kitchen maids do this to the stable hand she liked.

They had kissed and had hands on one another in interesting places before they broke apart because of someone rounding the corner.

She was with him on his side of the desk again. Virsin peered at the notes. Reports. Seemed like he was reviewing how well his farmers were doing.

He surprised her by turning to face her and placing the papers on his desk. He kept his hand over them, as if she were the wind about to disturb them. "Enough. Aren't you tired of this?"

"I am. As should you be, husband. Duties should be the first on our minds, and last, don't you think?" She trailed a palm up his chest, noticing his body tense, and he rolled as if about to sit on the desk.

Something clanked, and she glanced down to make sure he hadn't spilled ink everywhere, but nothing was amiss. She resumed her chase. She leaned into him, fitting herself against his form. Her hand slid up to his tie, fingers about to wrap around it when she had nothing.

Two steps she stumbled back before catching herself on his chair and tumbling over the arm to sit heavily on it. "Regus!"

"Forgive me." He cried, grabbing her hands and pulling her up.

Once she was on her feet, he slid a hand around her waist, while the other kept her hand in his. Was he about to dance with her? She smiled, fitting back against him again. His belt felt thicker against her lower abdomen, with something larger in the middle.

He departed, rejecting her touch, using the desk as a barrier. He snatched his papers and sat in a narrow, plush chair reserved for those he did business with at his workspace.

Frustration leered and had Virsin rounding the desk after him. She grabbed his wrists, pushing them up above their heads as she pressed a knee in beside him in the seat. The arm of the furniture painfully digging into her thigh. The belt was in the perfect spot, with nothing between them as she desired. Why was his buckle so large today?

"Regus, please. I know you are attracted to me. You flush and get frustrated with my antics. Sometimes you look at me and I wonder if you're thinking about kissing me... and I want you to. Desperately." Virsin pressed her forehead against his.

His body stiffened under her, and his hips lifted as if he were about to unseat her.

Virsin hissed as the arm sank more into her thigh.

Regus' eyes grew wide, his hands pulled out of hers, and he had his palms and papers on her hips. "How did I harm you? Where? Forgive me. I-"

She shook her head, "Never mind that." She slid her fingertips over his cheeks, then trailed her index finger on his fuller bottom lip.

His breath caught; mouth parted. *Was he going to kiss her, finally? Should she take the initiative? Probably.*

Virsin slid her arms around his neck and tilted her head. Before he could somehow disappear from her again, she fit her lips to his. *A second kiss! She was touching him! Kissing him! What was she to do next? Another kiss? Would he run away?*

Perhaps he would show her how to use her tongue?

A faint cry sounded somewhere in the room. Odd. His hands crumpled the papers, fingers digging through them into her dress. A delicious hold indeed.

"Sin," he murmured against her lips. He covered them once more with his.

Definitely needed more of this.

There was the weird little whimper or whine again. *Wait? Was that her? Oh. Oh no. Was she supposed to make those sounds?*

Papers fluttered to the floor. His left hand spread, fingertips curling into the meaty part of her rear. The single paper in his hold disappeared. All she knew was his right palm was sliding up her back and his fingers tangled into her hair and, oh... there was his tongue.

His hips jerked with a grunt from him. It seemed as if he'd been struck. That thing... she realized now it was lower than his waist.

The kiss broke.

Virsin stared between them. It was hard. So hard. Was such a matter... normal? For it to feel like metal? She looked up at his face; he was pale. His breathing was in measured increments through his nose as his lips formed a thin line.

His hands circled her hips anew as he struggled to release them from the chair's tight space. "We cannot."

"Oh yes, we can!" She clenched her fists, but a change of heart followed. She put her hand over the hardness between his legs. Bravery was for the bold. Riches to the victors. Right? "You are re-" she blinked, exploring all around the cloth of his pants.

It was metal.

He was metal down there? He hadn't been that one night in his chambers.

"Wha..." Nothing in the books ever said anything about metal!

Chapter 25
You've Got to Know When to Borrow Strength

"It's a belt. Chastity." Reg groaned, rising to stand with her and pushing her away until she was against the lip of his desk. He continued to hold her, bent over, a death grip on her hips.

"A... what now?" Those words did not fit together. Nothing made sense. Regus and a kiss. Kisses. Kisses sent her toward a sensation she gave herself in the bath, but still at the dreadful ache stage. Belt. A thing to hold pants up, dresses down, things like that. And chastity?

Hindering words such as pristine and chastity was not to be anywhere near what they were about to do, and *were* doing.

"You are quite... I can't think of the word right now," Reg said to the floor, as he was still bent in half before her.

"Persistent?" There she had words. That one fit in the moment.

"Yes." His chuckle was breathy, as if he were fighting back a laugh, but his ribs were broken. "Persistent. I thought this would help me... help me not do what I do not mean to do."

The man shook his head. Some of his long hair fell from his bun as it waggled back and forth. So she smoothed it for him. Gathering the strands back to the cotton tie and holding them there.

The word hit her again. Chastity. Next, the other. Belt. Chastity belt.

"You're wearing a chastity belt?!" She jerked his head up with both hands, meeting him halfway even as he cursed.

"Ah... oh... don't do... Please don't pull. I almost had a level of calm and then..." He groaned, his face contorting.

She let go of his hair.

He breathed a sigh of relief, only to do his measured breaths again.

Virsin grabbed his mane and tugged.

Reg moaned, his mouth open, eyes half closed.

She liked that look.

But he grew paler and the muscles of his lower body seemed to twitch.

She pressed her lips together, gathering a deep breath as she watched his face go from somewhere between agony to a hint of pleasure, then back once more, but the pain was always deeper. "Let's remove it."

"No!" He hissed through his teeth, those half-lidded eyes slitting in anger.

"This is ridiculous!" Virsin cried, dropping her grip on his hair again. She crossed her arms over her chest. A seed of anger burst. "My own husband is wearing a chastity belt! Those are for priests and priestesses and those preachers and the pagan priests."

"Shamans."

"Right! The pagan shamans." She glared at the back of his head, because he was staring at the floor. Of course, he would help her with words even when he was in pain. Anything than to have the conversation she wanted to have.

She eyed the chair they were in. It was getting so good. He subsequently spoiled it. Again. Her eyes narrowed on the plush cushion. "Don't tell me this is why our cushions have more padding on them?"

"I didn't want to be any more uncomfortable than I already am. And sometimes I... it clanked."

She gritted her teeth, about to grab his hair again to make him look at her, but she also didn't want to hurt him. Her fingers grew into claws in the air and she shook them as if shaking him. Virsin took in another deep breath, filling her lungs and letting it out slowly. She relaxed her hands, cupping her cheeks with them, and gave herself one more calming breath. Following that, another.

"Regus. Brindle. Norvasos. Husband. Do you know how uncomfortable you have made me ever since our wedding night?"

Even she didn't recognize her own voice.

Reg looked up, his eyes darting from one to the other of hers, "I have?"

"I ache!" She threw her hands up. "All the time! It's like I'm always hungry, but no amount of food will do. I touch you and it's like getting a taste of my favorite thing. You are always nearly there, but then you go away. And I'm left still starving!"

"Virsin…"

"Oh, don't say my name! I get my hopes up even further when you do!"

"Wife?"

She glared at him over her fingers, trying to cool her cheeks with her palms.

"Right." He straightened, releasing her hips from his death grip. He cleared his throat, looking away as he adjusted his tie. His hand slid down and fixed the bulge, but not the right kind of bulge.

"I regret my decisions have reduced you to… a certain type of… starvation." Reg muttered to himself as he smoothed a hand over his hair. "I assumed you would find me detestable. My hands are rough, see?" He held them out to her, palms up.

"I like the sensation of them on my face and probably will elsewhere." She quickly debunked his worry.

"We know naught of each other."

She rolled her eyes. "Isn't that what we're supposed to do? Together? Get to know one another?"

A muscle in his jaw worked. Then he opened his mouth, only to close it again. "I am not a good man."

"And some old wrinkled thing who likes younger women and all in between, is? Or the Count, whose wrath I'd face should I speak? Or the Marquis that has three children with his mistress, but won't marry her because he wants to marry into money? Are those what you wanted me to wed instead of you?"

"Rather specific in the details, Virsin." Reg chuckled.

"Because those were my other choices. Not that I really had a choice. It was a list. You happened to be at the top because my cousin put you there." She crossed her arms over her chest, leaning back against the desk to regard him. Did he not know? Of course not. She'd never seen him at court. Or any of the balls, or anything.

"They haven't killed, at least." Regus watched her, his face an emotionless void.

One. Single. Solitary point against him. She couldn't imagine anyone taking a life. But it was for their country. To keep everyone safe. "Did you enjoy it?"

His stonelike facade faded ever so slightly into something like disgust, "No. Not at all."

"You're still better than the others, to me."

Was this all she had to do? Tell him her options other than him? Why hadn't she thought of this before?

"I see." Reg paced before her. He talked after turning twice, "I'm still going to save you for the man after me. Like I said, I want to show him respect."

"Those are the men after you."

"No. No, they are not!" Reg snapped, stilling in front of her with a wildness to his countenance. "I will find better."

"Where?" she spat, getting in his face. "Are you going to pull some angel from the heavens? Make a priest negate his celibacy vow? I tell you right now, if the priest has one mole, that's a no."

Reg chuckled, "You don't like moles?"

"No! They..." she made a face, "They cause sickness."

"What if I have a mole?" Reg asked.

She gasped, "Do you?"

He laughed, and shook his head, "Not unless it's in the middle of my back for me to never see it."

"Shall I check?"

Reg's brows rose. "Persistent indeed." He sighed, "It will have to wait."

Was that a yes? Finally?!

"We have the ball. Afterward, I must leave for the east."

"What?" Virsin looked at the papers on his desk. She noted the edge of a bit of red wax under some. It resembled the bottom of the king's seal.

"Another small rebellious group is harassing a few villages." Reg lifted a shoulder.

"What about tonight?"

Reg shook his head. "I highly doubt I will find pleasure after being... strangled." He cleared his throat and looked away.

"Oh, right."

Chapter 26
Balls and Spears

"Is my favorite cousin with child yet?"

Virsin flinched, as Reg nearly toppled forward from his deep bow before their rulers. "Not at this time, my queen."

"Well?" Queen Lythaine said with a huff, "What are you waiting on? I brought many into the world hoping the youngest would be raised alongside one of yours, as I was with you, Duchess Victory."

Virsin heard the small strangled noise at her side as they straightened. It wouldn't be so terrible, but they were presenting themselves to their king and queen, in a large ballroom, with all the court ladies and gentlemen, and the entire army and their wives. Queen Lythaine did not know how to speak without projecting her voice loudly, either.

"My dear," the King patted his love's hand with a slight chuckle, "Afford them time. We might give them another try to meet, eh?"

"Yes, sounds like a plan, my love."

The look shared between them made nearly the entire ballroom blush.

"Besides, I have a job my Duke Victory is needed for in the east. Perhaps in the throes of his return, we shall hear the good news."

Reg stammered, "I sh-... it is... is..." He bowed sharply and turned on his heel to melt into the crowd of his regiment.

"It is an order, my dear Duke!" the queen called sweetly after him. Then she rose from her throne and grabbed Virsin by the wrist. "Come." The woman made the trek across the room easy as all parted before her as if she were a thrown spear. Lythaine dragged her through a set of doors to the right of the ballroom. On the balcony, her cousin released her once the attendants closed the doors behind them.

"Now, cousin, did you take the herbs I sent you to induce fertile lands?"

Virsin groaned, "Lythie, can we not talk about this?"

"Why ever not? I am quite experienced and might give you tips. Even show you positions. I allow some of my servants to pose for me to see if it will work before the king and I-"

"Lythaine!"

"Oh, fine." She grinned, then pursed her lips and tapped her cheek with a manicured finger. "So? Is he... handsome everywhere?"

"Yes, I suppose."

The queen narrowed her eyes. "Virsin, what are you not telling me?"

"We... we have yet to... do the things we should as husband and wife."

"You're still a virgin?!"

Virsin shushed the woman, feeling the heat from furnaces build in her cheeks, neck, and chest.

"Why ever not!?" the woman bellowed, hands on her hips and face in Virsin's.

"He... it's ridiculous, really." Virsin tried to think of a way to phrase it without it sounding too preposterous.

"Oh. Oh my, Virsin dear... is he damaged? Did one of those barbarians harm him and he cannot perform all the time?"

Yes. There was an escape. Perfect. Regus might preserve his image. And she could, too.

"It's not permanent! It's a wound to his... hip. Deep. And then there was an infection. But he is on the mend. Soon, I'll... we will... you know."

"I see." Her cousin's face filled with pity, "Oh my poor dear, Sin. Chin up. You won't be able to beat him off you, not that you would want to, I dare say." The Queen giggled knowingly, while hugging Virsin to her.

The rest of the ball was a blur of dancing with Regus, and sitting to talk with her cousin, or some of the other ladies. She couldn't remember much of the conversations, too worried she would slip and the queen would pick out her lie. Late into the morning, she slumped in their carriage as soon as it cleared the palace gates.

"Tired, my lady?" Regus asked from his seat across from her.

"Tremendously so," Virsin whimpered and looked away. "What of you, husband?"

"Not tremendously so," he said in a mocking tone, smiled when she stared at him. "Pity we are to get back in plenty of time, too."

"Enough time to what?" Virsin asked, hoping it wouldn't be anything too strenuous. Her bed was calling for her, and they still had an hour to go before even entering his lands on the other side of the city.

He shook his head. "Sleep a little before I need to depart."

"Oh." That sounded good. "At least you will gain some rest before the lengthy ride."

"Yes, unlike I originally imagined." He nodded with a jerk of his chin. "Yes, this is preferable."

Virsin thought it strange, how he spoke, but was far too tired to pick it apart in her usual way.

Not long after he said the word 'preferable,' Virsin closed her eyes. She must have fallen asleep, for she did not stir until the horses stopped. She watched Reg dismount from the carriage, then turned and gathered her into his arms before she attempted to exit.

"This is nice."

Regus chuckled. "Go back to sleep. Your maid will probably wake you up to get you out of this dress."

"Nn, or you may."

"You are far too tired." Reg murmured, but she didn't catch it.

Chapter 27
Resolve Dissolves or Solidifies

This reminded him of the war. Thousands of enemies, fire eating trees and buildings all around them, and his men flanking each other and him in various states of agony or glee. He jerked his sword up into the man Bertran tossed his way, halving him, and feeling the blood spatter warmly over his face and arms.

Fedvich faltered to his right as three attacked him. The redhead was barely dodging and blocking the array of strikes. "Vich!"

He sank his sword into another man who rushed him, twisting his body and hauling the man on his blade over his shoulder, flinging him toward the redhead. Fedvich crouched low enough to nearly lay on the heat baked soil. The dead weight hit two of the three, crushing them. Fedvich launched back into the fray, slitting the throat of the third before striking through the leather plates of the two flailing under the dead body before they even hit the ground.

Reg chuckled a little as Fedvich did a hair flip and the man rushing the redhead paused, eyes widening in lust or wonder right before they glassed over when Fedvich thrust his sword up through his chin.

"Let's not do that again, Fedvich. I can't be hard all over." Harry cried, slashing out with his whip, as he shot a bolt out of the crossbow he'd stolen from one of their dead enemies.

Regus glanced to his back at the boy who stood in the middle of their circle. Protected, but given the opportunity to maim those the warriors didn't fully kill. He hated the boy had to kill. They had worked so hard not to have another generation subjected to war, but here they were. Still at it. Remnants of the tyrant's regime persisted, pursuing domination.

He wondered if any of them knew who stood at his side.

"Better hard all over than to not be here mentally." Slayth growled, a slap of blood against Regus' cheek following the words.

Regus made a face, hating when Slayth controlled blood to hit him. He was covered in enough of it. "Who has their mind somewhere else?"

"Ooooh! That's right! The ball! Was she pretty?" Harry crooned, while each word was punctuated by the snaps of his whip taking the eyes out or ears off their enemies. Every one of those he let pass for Doxy to finish off.

It took them three days to get to this pocket of hell. Why hadn't Harry asked him then? "She was."

"Details, man!"

Regus rolled his eyes, swinging his sword in a wide arc and slicing through five men while knocking a sixth into Bertran's fist. "It was a dress. It was hot. The palace was bright and full of people gawking. What more is there?"

"Gods, he's not worth talking to about beauty." Fedvich muttered at his side, looking like he was dancing instead of killing, his swords flashing in twirls and slices.

"Does not having every gem explained bother you that much?"

Fedvich snorted, "I see the end. I wish to reach it before another wave magically appears."

It was true. There were few enemies left. Stragglers and wounded crawled away. Healthy ones ran; tails tucked between their legs. The two hundred men that made up his army took care of them, closing in the gap and circling the seven. He stepped back, placing a hand on Doxy's shoulder and turning the boy to face him. He studied each inch, noting the few scrapes. "Good job."

Doxy grinned, panting, and his mop of hair plastered to his forehead and neck.

"Gods, next time, let's go back to the snow, yeah?" Harry groaned, prodding Charn in the side with the end of his whip.

Charn nodded, watching the fire lick up the side of a tree and into the branches.

The small orchard was lost, but some of the village survived. Regus studied the area, making sure there weren't any surprises waiting for them. It looked like they didn't have any fatalities on their side. That was always a great feeling welling up in his chest. Survival.

"You're a god, aren't you, sir?"

Regus raised a brow as he sank the tip of his sword into the ground and leaned on it. What was his name? Eth? Elf? Something like that. "I am not."

"Lies!" Harry and Fedvich cried at the same time.

He shook his head as Harry wrapped an arm around the man and began explaining his lineage. Which Harry knew nothing of and completely made up as evidenced by the god of bigger dicks and goddess of war. It was one of the few secrets he kept from his Seven, and he would take it to his grave.

"I wonder if your blood will make that baby as pretty as your wife, but as strong as you."

Regus turned, staring into the light eyes of Slayth. The blood elf was the only one that could know where he came from, for Slayth had been his father's and grandmother's and great-grandfather's right hand. "See for yourself when Virsin has a child." *That is not mine, but her beauty should prevail, no matter the man.*

Chapter 27
F*ing, F, F... F

Two weeks. Two weeks of literally and figuratively kicking herself for falling asleep when she could have finally... had a ride. The conversation stuck in her mind like a dream. But she knew it was real.

Because such was her luck.

Opportunity. What she had been working so hard toward crashed in a snore because she was 'too tired.' Too tired!

It was fine. For the first week. She didn't fear his desire for her would disappear. Virsin hoped he wouldn't have a chance to change his own mind back to the ridiculous chastity thing.

After ransacking his chambers, she found the contraption under his bed and had studied it for quite some time. It seemed far too small for what she remembered seeing that one precious night. In addition, he mentioned strangulation.

She'd thrown it out.

Good riddance.

As she rearranged the library a bit, because she'd bought new books, she found a dilapidated shelf in the far corner. Versin located a book under and behind other dusty tomes. It had diagrams. Detailed ones. She retrieved the belt from the bushes north of the property, the dumping ground for things unsuitable for animal feed. She'd washed it twice, then put oils on the leather, and cleaned the metal like she'd done the men's armor again.

If the way he reacted to pulling his hair was replicated elsewhere... she'd need him to be tamed to reenact some diagrams.

Where had books such as this been when she had time to read three novels a day? She could have studied it several times and had it memorized. As it were, when he got back and they did normal things, whatever was normal, she would have to keep checking the book similar to cooking a new recipe.

Certain roles would then prove uncomfortable.

His arrival, if like past instances, would be closer to midnight. This time, she opted not to stay in his bed. In fact, she was rather proud of herself; she didn't plan any elaborate attacks.

He was ready. Finally. She hoped she wouldn't make a right fool of herself.

She felt the rush of adrenaline when she heard Mervas call from the foyer that the men were back a touch after noon. She quickly wiped her mouth off, dusted her dress for any crumbs as she half walked and half skipped the distance between the dining room and entrance.

Regus was already mounting the steps when she reached the open doors.

"My lord husband, welcome home." She said, not able to contain the giddiness she was sure was making her appear a fool.

"Wife. It is good to be home." He said with a genuine smile and a glowing countenance.

Harry dismounted at the stairs, too. Strange. He usually went with the men to the barracks. Glancing at her husband, she saw no wounds that would require Harry's support. "Lord Harry, welcome."

"My lady." Harry greeted her, the look on his face was as confused as she felt.

"Come." Regus said, motioning them into the house, "Mervas, are you well? Call for some tea for the office, will you?"

"I am, my lord, thank you. Of course, right away." Mervas answered with a bow before heading toward the kitchen.

"I must speak with you two. I wanted Slayth present, but he has pressing matters; of what nature I know not." Regus shook his head, leading the way through the house and up the stairs to the office.

"Shouldn't you like to rest, or wash first?" Virsin asked, a little concerned about this talk they were about to have. She glanced over her shoulder at Harry and caught his eye. He lifted his shoulders, still looking as anxious as she.

"No need. We can afterward."

She followed her husband into the office, perching on the sofa where he motioned. Harry settled across from her. Regus pulled blank sheets of paper out of the middle drawer of the desk before sitting down behind it. Reconsidering, he stood again and took his place beside her on the couch.

He didn't touch her, not even a knee to knee.

Mervas bought in tea and lemon biscuits, served them, and left.

Regus began, "I have a solution to our predicament." He grinned, looking between the two of them as if they should know the exact problem he spoke of.

"Problem?" Harry asked when Regus didn't say anything else.

"Yes!" He turned toward her, finally clasping his hands over hers in her lap. "Once I pass, Harry shall take you as his bride. He doesn't mind we kissed."

Silence filled the room.

Regus smiled, still.

Harry's mouth dropped in increments as his brows rose in the same measure.

"Gods save me." Virsin found herself muttering. Her body was doing some interesting things. Stomach flips, heart dropping, anger setting her chest aflame, tears burning in her eyes, and her hands trembled. "I thought we were beyond this. Harry, did you suggest this?"

"No!" He bellowed, then coughed lightly, "No. Not at all." He shook his head, sitting on the edge of the couch, "Was this your reasoning behind those questions last night? The ones about women?" The redhead groaned and smacked his forehead with his palm, "No wonder Slayth found five excuses not to be here, even when you ordered him to."

"Slayth is after you, should something bring your death."

"He's had four wives." Virsin said through gritted her teeth. "No. No. No." She shook her head, trying to get the other words screaming around in her brain to come forth other than no. "We were beyond this! I was going to ride you tonight!"

"Oh, I should go." Harry stood.

"Sit!" Regus barked, and Harry did as he was told in an automatic drop of his body. "If you still desire intercourse, he should do, as he will be your husband."

Silence. Again.

"Wha-what?" Virsin tried to make sense of it all.

"No. No." Harry threw his hands up. He stood, towering over Regus. He grabbed his lord up by the lapels, his face as red as his hair, "You are to make your wife happy. On your own."

Harry released him. Regus teetered on his own feet, before straightening, he looked the redhead in the eye, "You will take on this responsibility. You are my second. In every way now."

"Stop." Virsin stood, too, feeling left out. "I say, that is true. Second in all respects. Should anything happen to you, maybe I will marry Harry." She held back the shudder at the thought. "But he's probably going to have a wife of his own, right? Soon?"

"Yes." Harry growled, still staring down his lord as if envisioning Reg's death by his bare hands. "Order or not, this is not happening. Throw me out of the regiment if you cannot see reason. If you continue this madness."

"But it's a perfect plan. You don't have to wed a silly woman. You adore Virsin, yes?"

"As YOUR wife!" Harry spat.

Regus sighed, deflating slightly. "Am I to assume no one is to care for her when I die?"

Harry's lips thinned as his jaw muscles worked. In a drawn-out breath was an equally long curse, "Of course she will be looked after. Your Seven are here for her as much as we are for you. Not to mention everyone in this house, Mervas and Fince. So fuck her every day. Every minute. Be happy. Give Slayth a little one to spoil since he's not allowed to hype up his own. Let him drive you crazy by giving the kid sweets. Give Charn someone else to make fun of his voice and child-like fingers. Alright?"

Regus turned his gaze on Virsin. "I want to protect you."

Virsin rolled her eyes, "Your dick won't kill me."

Chapter 28
Does A Dick Kill? Asking For a Friend

Contrary to popular belief, no one kicks men when they are down. He drowns himself in his own sorrows and tries to make his wrongs worse all on his own. Virsin thought she might begin a study on males. After all, her husband was the strangest among them.

He had no vices. Other than a fetish for keeping his penis out of his own wife. Regus had some rage issues, but he confined them to the battlefield, as he should. He was well mannered, clean, and intelligent.

Regus didn't even fart at the dining table.

After their talk with Harry, Virsin was prepared to welcome him as a wife should her husband the moment the redheaded second departed their company. Upon seeing her husband's countenance, she knew such was not to happen. Nor would it happen that night, nor the next day, nor the next.

Then the worst appeared. A woman's body sensed the right moment to ruin things. For five days, she kept to her chambers, cursing her luck or lack thereof.

On the sixth day, Virsin ventured out after confirming her vengeful body had stopped spilling her hard-earned blood. Not widely. To satisfy her sweet tooth, she went to the kitchens, then to the library to put back the seven books she had read and select new ones for her nightstand. Regus was out.

Of course he was.

The seventh day, oh the day of holy numbers, Virsin found her husband in the sweltering afternoon at the training grounds. The men loved the fresh water with lemon and lime slices. She brought a basket of fruit and salted pork to help replenish their bodies, too.

She walked to her husband, who stood a few paces away from the tables where his men partook of her gifts. The sight of him wiping the sweat from his brow and neck made her mouth salivate. Not that she needed reminding, but she found herself desperate to finally possess him.

"Are you well, my wife?" Regus asked once she was close.

Virsin followed the trail of a bead of sweat down one of his pectorals with a single fingertip. Too entranced to notice the question. Until he asked it again, and the amused tone to his usually grave voice broke her out of her trance. "Oh, I am."

"I see." His brows rose as the same finger to touch him was touching her lips. "I uh… thought we might have a change in scenery for our dining tonight. Would you like to dine alone with me?"

Yes! "What kind of scenery did you have in mind, husband?" She looked up, searching his gaze, and felt the familiar flutter in her heart.

"My chambers." He answered, leaning down to place his lips closer to her ear.

"Yes!" She covered her mouth, a gasp escaping her lips right after the screamed acceptance.

Regus laughed, rubbing his ear, "I suppose I should surprise you with more scenery soon, too."

Dinner was slow to arrive. Minutes were years. Hours were decades. She altered her attire three times. The cook revealed nothing regarding the meal destined for the master's chamber. Changed her dress again. Paced. Loosened her cords before Bea sat her down and told her to be a lady. Bea pulled those laces tighter than normal as punishment. She was unaware impatience and changing dresses were so unlady like.

At last, Bea sent her to his chambers. Her palms sweated. Her lungs refused to work properly. There was a heart in her throat and one thrumming in her core. The dress she chose was wrong. She needed to go back and change again.

"Virsin." His voice warmed her as Bea shoved her into the room and locked the doors behind her. Rude. Unnecessary and rude.

"Regus." She answered, swallowing down some of the excess water in her mouth at seeing him.

He was in his black pants; she didn't know if he owned any other color, really. His shirt was a dark blue, nearly matching his eyes, and it was open enough to reveal a portion of his chest to remind her about touching it at the training grounds earlier. Decades ago.

"Come here." He said, the order snaking under his usually kind tone to her. Regus held two wine glasses.

Food was nowhere to be found. She would have to reprimand the cook for being late, later. How dare she undermine their night. Virsin walked over to him, not even thinking of a way to retort his demand. When she reached him, she saw the curtains flutter gently. The doors to the balcony were open.

He handed her a glass, then opened the curtain for her to step through.

The sunset gilded the forest and the small outlier buildings further west in golds and reds. The table was tiny, intimate, and set with two platters of fruits, meats, and cheeses. A light affair, but there was plenty of it.

Finger foods. Snacks. Enough to keep the energy up.

How thoughtful.

She swallowed down half the wine.

Regus chuckled, plucking up a piece of cheese and a dried cranberry, "Eat before you drink more. I will not have you intoxicated for this."

Again, the order in his tone made her defiance rise, "I'm not drunk." She said before taking the snack from his fingers with her lips. She chewed and swallowed, "I'm fully aware and will keep my wits about me for this, I assure you of that. I've waited too long."

"Oh have you, dearest?" Regus asked, "Duty is not something I take lightly, but I also want to honor and respect you. Your body... when I first saw you, I knew my resolve would be tested."

She studied him. The scar pulling his lips. The tan of his skin. His long hair was abnormal for nobility, and definitely for a warrior. The darkness of his eyes could swallow one's soul. He was intimidating, lethal, and yet she still felt the lust rise in a deep throbbing ache. But she also understood, even with the aggravation of him not willing to touch her, she was growing to love the man before her. His honor, his laugh, the way his features darkened more when she dared to do something which stirred him. Regus Brindle Norvasos, Duke Victory, Duke Vicious, her husband, was ready to let this relationship be what it could be.

"No more running away."

Regus' lips twisted as he swirled the wine he had yet to sip. "No more chasing after me half clothed unless in this chamber, or yours."

She scoffed, "I was fully clothed. Mostly."

"Mostly," Regus echoed, before taking a few swallows of his wine. He set the glass down. "Clothing should not be the standard at the moment."

That look. That was different. It made her gasp and tremble. The unknowing virginal part of her spouted, "Is this going to kill me, after all this time?"

He chuckled, slipping his fingers into her dipping neckline and jerking her into him. His free hand found the slit of the old-fashioned dress and pressed around her upper thigh like a warm brand. "You may think you will die of pleasure, but I assure you, I shall bring you back to the brink, only to throw you over again."

Chapter 29
Of Magic Tongues

The glass slipped from her fingers. As soon as it shattered on the stone of the balcony, he scooped her up into his arms. His lips broke her gasp.

"You are quite dangerous. And wasteful. It was the good wine." He murmured, his cheek rubbing hers before he sucked her earlobe in his mouth.

The sensation of his teeth had her whimpering. She wrapped her arms tight around his neck. "I guess we will have to call for another bottle."

"You can have mine. I'll be sipping from you for a while." Regus' words were soft in her ear as he carried her through the curtains and back inside. His boots crunching on a few shards of glass.

"What does that mean?" She wondered if it was the thing the male lead did to the female lead in her romance books. The licking. Down there.

He sat on the bed, then collapsed on it. His firm hands pulled her skirt all the way to one side. "Move up." He urged her by gripping her ass and pulling.

"But..." she did as she was told, waddling forward on her knees.

Regus growled, sitting up again, her rear still in his hands. He slid one arm under her, then the other. With a grunt, he lifted.

She scrambled to find a grip; sure he was about to truly throw her across the room. Her fingers dug into his hair, and she hooked her knees around his shoulders.

His breath was... oh.

Why did he have to be so impatient he lifted her so precariously to his shoulders while a perfectly safe bed was under them? She squealed when he fell back again, her calves pinned under his back, her arms trapped under herself as her fingers were still tangled in his hair. Her squeal automatically cut off by the softness of his bedspread. She couldn't breathe. Could he? His face was buried between her legs, surely... a moan escaped as she felt his fingers working the fabric of her drawers. A rip abruptly sounded.

His breath truly did warm her then.

Virsin wriggled, trying to get her hands free. A wet warmth replaced where the open seams of her underwear had been. Her hips jerked up. His grip clamped over her ass and pulled her back down.

"Hold still." He demanded under her.

She did as she was told. Her squirming ending with two words and being trapped over him. What on this earth was he doing?

Again, a warmth slid up her slit. So slow. Her whole body trembled. Then the same warmth enveloped the bump she rubbed in the bath. Virsin nearly came up off the bed. Only his ministrations and shoulders trapping her kept her from doing that.

Gasping, she twisted, attempting to liberate her hands. One hand free, she slid it up only to stop. Another swipe, then another, had her closing a fist in the bedspread.

The books didn't do this justice.

Faster than what she could do with her fingers, the euphoric orgasm rose and washed over her. His tongue slid in when she shook with her second ever release, and she swore under her breath as he drank from her. It was as if he'd never stop with his tongue inside her.

His hands crept up under her, pressing into her ribs. He sat her up, settling her on his chest.

Virsin looked down at his scarred face between her thighs and pulled her dress off his mouth and nose. She watched him lick his lips, and something about such a simple action made her wetness drip more. "I... what was that? How did you learn it?"

"I was worried I wouldn't be any good." Regus turned his head, pressing his chin into her thigh before he kissed it. His lips parted, and he mouthed her leg before kissing it again. He nuzzled into her, looking up at her with one eye, "I learned from Fedvich. He showed me... well it was on a melon..." He chuckled, "I thought him mad, but I guess he wasn't."

"No, I don't think he was." Virsin agreed, fanning herself with both hands. "How should I... can you teach me to do... something as good as that for you?"

He made a sound in his throat as he turned his head to stare up at her. "One day. I'm easy to please." He smiled up at her as he asked, "Ready for another?"

Without waiting for her answer, he pulled her over his face. This time, his fingers joined in on the action and Virsin swore she was about to burst into a million pieces. Six times over.

She lay on her side, sprawled over his bed. She couldn't get enough air in her, stop trembling, nor quell the twitching and pulling of her chasm. Sorcery. He had magic. Had to.

His hands slid over her after he detangled himself from her skirt and legs. He moved her more toward her stomach. She felt so heavy, yet weightless. She knew she couldn't move. Running away would be impossible if his dick were to fatally harm her.

The dress loosened. The corset. She could breathe. Why hadn't she removed the contraption before?

Right. Her brain was with his tongue when he was under her. A sound he made drew her attention back to him.

He sat on his knees, his dark gaze trailing over her. Reg leaned forward, resting on a hand. He dragged the thin sleeve off her shoulder. His lips trailing in their wake down to her elbow. Then he turned her to her back, did the same to the other side.

His eyes captured hers as he lifted one of her legs and let it fall to the other side of him. He settled on his knees, which pressed against her inner thighs. His fingers trailed over her belly, up between her breasts, and hooked into her dress. Regus pulled, loosening the dress from where it was caught over her corset. He lifted the contraption, freeing her of it and tossing it over the edge of the bed.

Regus sighed, his attention on her chest. "I've dreamed of those. And your thighs." He said while squeezing them in both hands.

Virsin tried to lift her hands to cover her breasts, but the dress hooked over her elbows holding her arms hostage. She barely managed to conceal them with her fingers. A far cry from wrapping them over them as she wanted.

It was his eyes that made her pause. There was a hunger which seemed to erupt in them when she touched herself. Or was it jealousy? Not sure how to proceed, she worked her bottom lip between her teeth. Again his gaze changed, shifted, looking at her mouth before dropping back down to her breasts.

The hands on her thighs were gripping and loosening as if he were judging the firmness of them.

Did he want that from her?

She moved her hands similarly. It was nice. But not as nice as his warm palms on her legs. Still, it elicited a sound from him akin to the whimper of an animal.

His hand slid between her legs. Again, his digits slipped into her.

Virsin gasped, her grip tightening on herself.

He moaned and pressed his thumb between her nether lips and onto her clit. He worked his hand in such a way his fingers slid inside while his thumb rubbed her clit. Magic. Magic indeed.

Chapter 30
What Is This? This White Stuff Everywhere?

"Virsin."

She gazed at the man who had driven her to madness and was preventing her from slipping off the cloud.

"I don't think I can..." He groaned, then pulled his fingers from her.

Her gaze dropped to his hands on his groin. The bulge there. Quickly, he flipped the buttons through and his manhood stood between them. That's what the books wrote about.

"Forgive me." He said as he leaned over her. Reg held his cock, and the thickness parted her as his fingers brushed over her. Then his hand was on her hip, and he sank into her sheathing himself.

Regus' breathing was as ragged as hers, but he held still. "Bring your knees up, Sin." A darkness permeated his voice.

She did as she was told, and he slid deeper. She moaned and whimpered, rocking against him as she had his fingers. Virsin couldn't believe how decadent he felt.

Wasn't this supposed to hurt?

"I hope... I hope you are fine? Good? Well?" He groaned, "Because... if you move thus... I cannot stop."

"I am well." She breathed, gripping his sides because that's as far as the dress sleeves would allow her.

"Good." He settled over her, crushing her slightly. "Hold on."

She didn't have to ask why, nor have time to.

His hips moved in a rhythm she could liken to him upon his horse coming up the lane. Quick and sure. He kissed her, obliterating all thought. He filled her below and sampled her above. How was this so delicious?

Regus was everything at this moment. All she experienced. All she wanted to feel. And dammit, why was this dress still on?

She lost count of his thrusts. Just as she was about to ascend another cloud, he grunted and pulled out. Warmth pooled on her stomach where his cock was now trapped between them.

After a few grunts, shudders, and a sigh, Regus hoisted himself up on his hands and knees.

She looked down between her breasts and saw a white pool trickling down the curve of her belly and a longer spurt toward her chest. She grazed it with a fingertip. Touched what was on her finger to her thumb, then extracted her arm out of her dress to bring her hand closer.

It was an odd consistency.

She licked it.

"Were you… told to do that?" Regus asked between pants as he sat back on his heels.

"No. Am I not to?" Virsin froze, sure she had done something wrong. Was a lady not supposed to touch the seed, just accept it where it went?

He looked up at the ceiling with a groan, "Woman, you shall be every death to me."

"Hardly. For this is life." She pointed to the pool of him on her belly. "And you've ruined this dress."

He chuckled, looking back down at her. "Very well. Duke Vicious, Ruiner of Virsin's Dresses." He gripped the garment, a hand on one side of the slit, and the other with the opposite. His hands jerked, spreading wide. The rip of fabric echoed in his chambers. Regus tossed the top of her dress off her, the rest pinned under her. "For there will be many more torn asunder, I assure you."

With those promising words, he ripped what little was left of her pantaloons and chemise, completely baring her to him.

His palms raked up and down her belly, over her thighs, and then slid back up to cup her breasts. He pinched her nipples between his thumb and forefinger, then squeezed what he could. His smile was wicked as she arched into his hands.

"Imagine, husband, how much time you must make up for what we have lost."

Regus' head canted to the side, his hair flopping with it, before he pulled the ties out of it and let the thick locks fall free. "Shall we begin now? What did I do? How foolish I was." He leaned over her, propping up on one elbow as his other hand slid between them to part her nether lips. "Should six orgasms a day suffice?"

"Hm..." She tried not to moan, but her hips rocked into him against her command to hold still. "Seven, for the interest."

He chuckled, "Seven, yes, of course, my lady wife."

She'd passed out. Virsin swore she did because she didn't remember falling asleep. She had no recollection of being tired.

Her whole being felt peculiar each time she descended from the last orgasm, only for Regus to recover his breath and start anew.

The man was stamina incarnate.

He was a manifested god.

He'd rendered her immobile, speechless, and thoughtless.

The newest sensation was the comfort of a warm body under hers as she lay sprawled over his scarred, bare chest. His deep breaths, punctuated by soft snores, made her eyebrow twitch; however, things could be far worse. He could breathe fire amid the snores.

She was sticky everywhere. Virsin was sure she was absolutely nasty. A horrid beast to look at.

She unhooked her foot from around his calf, groaning at how her muscles failed to cooperate by lifting her appendage. She raked her leg across his. Of course, the warrior was a light sleeper.

Regus clasped the back of her thigh and dragged her back into place. Then his hand slid up to cup her ass. He vocalized, wordlessly. Unless it was in some language she hadn't heard before.

"What?"

"Nnn," Regus answered, his body vibrating with the full length stretch.

Still his hand didn't leave her rear, his fingers splaying wide during the elongation to close back into his original hold. He did not reiterate whatever it was he had said before. It must not be important. Dream sleep. What was he to dream about with her in his embrace, she wondered.

Again, she tried disengaging.

Regus grumbled and pulled her over him. She slid up his chest as he brought a leg up between hers. Virsin sighed, scrambling to push herself up on wobbly arms.

His hips rocked, rubbing his thigh against her core.

She lifted her head, meeting his gaze. "What are you doing? I need to bathe." She smelled her own breath and slapped a palm over his nose to keep him from smelling it.

Regus flinched, "I did nothing to deserve a broken nose, Sin." He took her hand away, holding it in one hand as he rubbed his nose with another.

"I didn't break it."

He chuckled, "No, you didn't. You don't need to bathe. Not yet." He slid his hands down, cupping her torso with thumbs caressing the sides of her breasts. "My dear, I need a ride."

She whimpered, "I have not the strength."

He lifted her, sitting up with her. "No matter, nice and slow." He murmured, kissing her.

Virsin turned her head, making him kiss her cheek as she covered her mouth, "I have horrid breath."

"No, you don't." He took her coverage away again and grasped her chin with his free hand to hold her still as he kissed her. Slow. Languid, like the roll of his hips.

His shaft parted her as if it was more part of her than of her husband.

"Regus." She moaned, wondering at how wet she already was, or if she had ever gone dry in the night. She tilted her hips, and he slid his hands down to aid their union. Once inside, she rocked her body as best as she could.

She felt lazy.

Still Regus' breath quickened, and he lay back, holding her waist in his grip. His dark eyes were half lidded, and on her chest. "See, a bath now would be a waste."

Virsin let his hands guide her into a rhythm, meeting the slow undulations of his body under hers. Looking down at herself, she traced a hand over the area where she believed his seed had dripped onto her dress. She expected some evidence. But there was scarcely anything.

She trailed her palms over her breasts, expecting to touch the remnants of the trails his tongue made. Some stickiness remained, far less than initially anticipated. His hips began jerking up into her, and she noted his attention on her ministrations to herself.

He liked it when she touched herself. So she did, meeting his thumb as he slid it between them. Virsin held his hand as the rough pad caressed her clitoris.

Stamina incarnate, indeed, she thought as he pounded up into her, until she trembled and cried out. Another plunge nearly had her toppling off him, but he kept her seated, grunting after another thrust, and then pulling out to spill himself between them.

"Virsin, I shall take you for as long as I can. Make up for lost time." He said, breathless after his seed stilled its pulse.

"Good." Virsin leaned back, unable to move. A question arose, "Is it safe to do these things when I gain a child?"

Regus' hand paused in its languid caress of her thigh. "I fear... it will not be fair to a child to be of me."

Virsin peered down at him, making herself depart from her place against his leg to cup his face in her hands. She remembered the discussion of his childhood and felt her heart break. "If it is fear of leaving our child alone in case of your demise, they won't be."

Regus trailed his fingers through her hair, cupping her in both palms, "Perhaps I may be convinced by you, my love, one day. Make me see as you do, as you have convinced me to partake of you. I hope you don't embarrass me as you have with conversing about our sex life," he said with a small chuckle. "Though, I believe I am still a fool."

Chapter 31
Vicious Insatiability

She learned not to dress in too many layers. Impatience and appetites reigned. She declined more engagements than she accepted.

Carriages were not ideal for hard dicks and wet lips.

They purchased more robes. He learned how to make her scream his name, and how much teasing it took for her to launch herself at him. He mastered delegating tasks to stay by her side.

She gained stamina, and he gained a love for life.

"Dear gods, put her breast away." Harry cried, turning and nearly braining himself on the closing door as he walked into the office. He stumbled back, catching himself on the couch opposite them.

Virsin looked up at her husband as she lay on him. His hand, fingers inside her corset top, covered her. She mimicked the roll of his eyes and lopsided smirk before kissing him and slipping out of his lap. "Very well, Harry, you may turn around. All is hidden from your virgin visage."

"Vir-" He gritted his teeth, still rubbing the blood red spot on his forehead as he turned to regard them with slitted eyes. "Having slipped and slid on his dick for weeks doesn't entitle you to label me as virginal in any manner. I'd rather not look, and have my eyes gouged out by Vicious turning Jealous."

"You had your chance to take your virginity and change it with her." Regus muttered, taking the papers Harry offered him, not even bothering to get up or straighten from his lounging position on the couch. He skimmed the report, toying with a strand of his wife's hair as she was still within reach. "How are you handling your new work load?"

"My lord," Harry spoke through his teeth, "It is time you stop thinking with your cock and rejoin the public. And you well know I am not a pure man."

"That bad?" Regus studied his second over the papers, giving Virsin's strands a playful tug.

She hid her smirk behind her hand, enjoying the scene, and how her husband was teasing more than just her.

Harry threw up his hands, pacing back and forth near the couch, "Slayth won't listen to a single order I give him. Charn screams at the new recruits every five seconds, which makes them fall over laughing until the next time he does it. Doxy is whining and moping around. Fedvich was missing for three days only for him to return constantly scratching his crotch. And Bertran relaxes and tells me to handle everything."

"How is that different from any other day?" Regus asked, his face stone.

The second in command slowed his pace, turned on his heel like he was winding up a toy, and licked his lips as he placed his hands on the back of the couch. "I shall tell you, this is not a laughing matter. I found a gray hair! Several!" He pulled his hair down from the braid twisting around his head, showing a few gray lines within the vibrant tendrils.

"Oh, you've had those." Virsin waved a hand dismissively, only to snort, trying to hold back a giggle as his eyes turned wild.

"I'll trade." Harry nodded, "I'll keep Duchess Insatiable entertained while you whip the men into place." He kept nodding, eyelids still wide, "I'll find something in the shape of your penis and let her chew on it all day. I don't care."

"Duchess Insatiable?" Virsin glanced at her husband who lifted a shoulder, "And I'll have you know I don't chew things of size; I cut them into bite-sized pieces." Her aim was perfect as both men winced.

Harry composed himself and said, "Please, return."

Regus sighed, tossing the report onto the table between the couches, "I suppose I shall have to return to watch over the kids sometime."

"He can handle another week." Virsin said, fluttering her lashes as she kept her attention on Harry. She grinned as he grew pale. "Oh fine, we cannot ignore our chores forever."

"Tomorrow." Regus' tone returned to its normal bite as his eyes turned to Harry.

"I'm holding you to your honor bound words. Even if I must drag you off her first thing in the morning and toss you naked in the training grounds..." Harry warned.

"He's gotten rather bold, hasn't he, lord husband?"

"Bold indeed." Regus answered, his brow quirking. "I believe my wife was correct. You have the wherewithal to handle the men for another week."

"No!" Harry slapped his hands against the ornate wood of the couch edge. "No, sir!" He added at Regus' glare, then swallowed. "I shall see you tomorrow, my lord." He bowed, then practically ran out of the door before Regus could say a word.

Virsin giggled as she asked, "Are they truly that terrible to him?"

Regus' lips twisted into a grin. "Yes. Only because he is easy to rile. If he didn't fight back every step of the way, they wouldn't disobey as much." He paused before adding, "I don't remember him having a stripe of gray hair, though. Did he have it before?"

"No, my love, but he needn't be told. His poor vanity has suffered enough, don't you think?" Virsin grinned, patting her husband on his chest.

"Insatiable." Regus murmured, taking her fingers in his. He toyed with slipping his fingers in and out of hers, "Better you than me, I suppose."

Virsin shook her head, frowning, not liking the title at all. "We will have to change it. Somehow."

He chuckled, kissing her fingers as he pulled her to him again. "Sin, it's time."

"Again? If they only knew they labeled the wrong one insatiable!" Virsin cried, but still arranged herself over him to kiss him deeply as his hands roamed.

The End

135

Acknowledgements

This book wouldn't be in your hands without you. Thank you for purchasing, reading, and supporting me. If you are a long-time fan, you are appreciated more than I can put into words.

My husband is the ever present, patient, cheerleader, and behind the scenes idea bouncer for all my books. I want to thank him, and my dear Kona, our adopted boxer dog, for being there. Your love is what makes these romances shine.

To my beta readers, you are absolutely adored. I couldn't do it without your support, and your 'huh?' comments on each document. Trust me, when I go back and read it through new eyes I go, 'huh?' sometimes, too.

My Husband Wants to Keep Me Dominant

Chapter 1: Whips and Cups

"Harder!" The slap of the leather upon flesh broke the rhythm of grunts, pants, and soft feminine cries. The leather thongs slid over the sweaty tanned back with red welts as the muscles gathered and released to pick up the order with gusto.

"Yes, Mistress," the redhead turned his head. His heated gaze pierced through the low candlelit room, resting on her as his body undulated fully to make his hips thrust his cock harder and deeper into the woman under him.

His audacity made her want him, but she must keep to her role.

And her chastity.

Striding forward, the heel of her riding boots clacking against the cracked wooden floorboards, she put the butt of the whip under his chin, turning his head up so he met her gaze. She placed a boot on his ass, after hiking her white skirts up to her knees to reveal the thick leather and a slash of pale thigh between.

His thrusts stilled, pressed fully into the woman beneath him who whimpered and mewled as she rocked her hips to keep her own pleasure alive.

She leaned down, putting her face in his, the nose of the mask poking his right cheek, "I told you to focus on your whore, sir."

"She's had an orgasm. Don't you want one, Mistress Garnet?" He asked, a glint in his dark eyes as his lips twisted to one side.

Her thoughts drifted to how his hand felt on the small of her back earlier when he'd ushered her into the room while holding the door open for them. The length of his cock before he'd sheathed it in Clover, how did it feel? "You haven't the money to take my first, sir. Nor do I think you're worthy since you cannot manage the simplest of orders. Clover, is he good enough for you?"

"Yes," Clover said with a moan, still undulating under the lord to make the sling slide him in and out of her.

She watched the muscles in his arms move with each swing, and knew he was helping Clover remain fucked despite his mistress halting them. Insubordinate. She gripped his long tresses and hauled back while keeping her foot on the left globe of his taut ass.

His hands flew to his hair as his back arched.

The lord's hiss of pain made her lick her lips. He had the best sounds of her clients. The best body, too.

"Mistress, I should warn you, there are tips..."

She felt them, a few biting into her palm. The mistress jerked his head further back, bending him over the length of her leg so the back of his head rested on the top of her knee-high boot. "I didn't permit you to speak so freely."

Clover took full advantage, gripping those narrow hips between her legs and riding her way to climax.

"No, Mistress. You did not." The redhead stated between pants.

Her partner cried out her release, and lay in the swing with a smile as she reveled in the orgasm.

"Finish yourself." She said, hovering over him before she felt her balance begin to tilt from the odd position. Her boot heel clacked back on the floor, and she grew steadier on both feet. He hadn't moved to obey. Instead, his eyes were up, watching her, hands still in his hair, fingers touching hers.

With a flick of her wrist, the leather thongs smacked his flat stomach, taught with the strain of bending over backwards. His body jerked, but he didn't make another move to comply. His tongue trailed over his lips, eyes still on her.

"May I speak, Mistress?"

She raised a brow, the mask tight because of how damp it had grown from her own sweat. "Should I allow him, Clover?"

"He might've a good idea, hm?" Clover's twang snaked out as she watched a spot on the ceiling, swinging gently in the straps of cloth hung from the rafters.

"Speak." She demanded, returning to stare into his dark eyes. There seemed to be a flare there, like they held their own fire amid the brown depths.

"Let my mouth give you an orgasm. It'd be better than your fingers after I leave." Another smirk twisted his lips, "Trust me."

"Since he's worthy of you, Clover, do you think I should sate his thirst?" She had to play the part. Keep to her act. No matter how this body looked or what he did to her nethers mattered.

The bastard knew she was wet. Who wouldn't be? All the whores fought for him. The rare redhead, the rarer long hair, and a body that promised all sorts of power. She was one of three Mistresses he hadn't broken.

"Oh aye."

Clover was no aid.

She felt her eyes narrow as he grinned. Already thinking he'd won. She smiled, and loosened her hold on his hair. Over the handle of the whip, she beckoned him with a finger as she took a step back.

He shifted, every muscle in his body taught as he turned from bending over backwards, to walking on his hands and knees before her.

The little room held the swing, the tiniest of desks, a wobbly chair, and a narrow couch with the back broken off. In another two steps, she bumped into the furniture. "Stay."

She waited until he stilled, sitting back on his heels, before disengaging her hand from his tresses. Slowly she gathered her skirts, all lace and cotton, and pulled them up to free her legs up to her knees. She threw her leg over the backless couch, straddling it, before sitting and leaning back against the threadbare arm. Her skirts were dangerously high, threatening the lord with a sight of the most private of her body.

She dropped her skirts, flicking the whip languidly at her side as her other hand trailed up her bare thigh, until the damp heat of herself pressed against the back of her thumb. "You've gone soft. Fix it."

He was quick to obey this time. His hand slaking down his Clover-orgasm slick cock. With a few pumps, and his dark eyes steady on her hand between her legs, his manhood revived, standing tall.

"Remove your hand, let me see."

Again, such quick compliance.

"Tell me, whipping boy, do you thirst?" She snapped the whip against the back of the couch, letting her arm rest above her head as she slid down the length of the couch. Every inch baring as much thigh, she stopped before her core could be viewed.

"I do, Mistress."

She liked that tone. The one where he was one the verge of breaking the little thread of control. A tiny shard of fear pricked through the adrenaline of having a man on his knees before her. What if she pushed him too hard and he did lose control? Could she keep him off long enough for Clover to regain control or for her to grab Nathan or Sawyer?

Would she still be intact by the end of the night? She should end this farce. But she didn't want to. It wasn't the end of the world if a husband found his new wife experienced, was it? If, and it was a large if, her father finally found himself face to face with a man he thought would do for his precious, only daughter. And her brothers didn't beat him to death.

"Mistress Garnet?"

Of the fuck gods, she'd gotten lost in thought. "Do you want to drink?" She flicked her fingers; her skirts still gripped in them shy of giving him a glance of the cup.

"Desperately."

Oh, that was bad. That look. The desperation in his voice.

She switched her gaze from him, better to clear her head, to Clover. The other woman nodded, and got up. Clover opened the door, and motioned.

Two large forms filled the doorway, then the room, following Clover in like shadows. Nathan was the broadest and tallest of the two, his bald head shining black in the candlelight, his shirt a stark contrast of white against ebony. Sawyer, while smaller, wasn't by much, and the metal plated gloves he wore took away any hopes patrons had of taking out the palest white man ever seen.

The Mistress held her hand up, stopping the men as Clover crossed the room to her side. She smiled up at Clover, "Remember that one time you helped Opal?"

Clover grinned, and settled herself beside Garnet.

"Stay there. Or they will end the show for you." She said, returning her gaze to the lord still on his knees before her.

"Wha..." he began, then stilled when Clovers fingers slid into where he wanted to be.

She arched and moaned as Clover's fingers found her clit and began rubbing in tight circles. Garnet kept her eyes on the lord, watching his breathing quicken, his muscles grow tight, his mouth work. And then his eyes drifted from where Clover pleasured her, to meet her gaze.

The shock threw her over the edge in a few more rough strokes as she stared into his eyes.

Clover giggled during her throes, and she shoved the woman toward the redheaded lord.

Losing her balance, Clover sprawled over the couch. The lord helped her up, only to grip her thighs, spreading them, and shoving her down into his lap. He pushed Clover back against the couch, as he gripped the edge of the aged furniture. He slid into her, and his dark brown flickering gaze met Garnet's as he pounded into a mewling Clover.

About the Author

Sam Wicker is a small town, Appalachian girl who grew up riding the line between family farm work and reading until her eyes hurt. She's married to the most loving husband ever, and together they have a fur-baby named Kona, a rescue, and the most adorable boxer-bulldog-cur mutt ever. Sam's always wanted to write stories full of romance, realistic people doing fantastical things, and animals that awe or make you go 'aww!' Her stories are meant to provide an escape, a laugh, a good think or two, and hope. She hopes that her stories inspire those suffering from anxiety, depression, and unfulfilled dreams. These stories are from someone much like you, so keep going, and make those dreams happen.

Be sure to follow her on Instagram, YouTube, and Twitch @WriterSamWicker

Website: https://carderwickerwriting.com